LIBERATION DAY

LIBERATION DAY

STORIES

GEORGE SAUNDERS

THORNDIKE PRESS
A part of Gale, a Cengage Company

Thorndike Press® Large Print Basic.
The text of this Large Print edition is unabridged.
Other aspects of the book may vary from the original edition.
Set in 16 pt. Plantin.

LIBRARY OF CONGRESS CIP DATA ON FILE.
CATALOGUING IN PUBLICATION FOR THIS BOOK
IS AVAILABLE FROM THE LIBRARY OF CONGRESS.

ISBN-13: 979-8-8857-8278-4 (hardcover alk. paper)

Published in 2022 by arrangement with Random House, an imprint, and
a division of Penguin Random House LLC.

Printed in Mexico
Print Number : 1   Print Year : 2023

FOR PAULA

CONTENTS

CONTENTS

LIBERATION DAY

It is third day of Interim.

A rather long Interim, for us.

All day we wonder: When will Mr. U. return? To Podium? Are the Untermeyers (Mr. U., Mrs. U., adult son Mike) pleased? If so, why? If not, why not? When next will we be asked to Speak? Of what, in what flavor?

We wonder avidly. Though not aloud. For there may be Penalty. One may be un-Pinioned before the eyes of the upset others and brought to a rather Penalty Area. (Here at the Untermeyers', a shed in the yard.) In Penalty, one sits in the dark among shovels. One may talk. But cannot Speak. How could one? To enjoy the particular exhilaration of Speaking, one must be Pinioned. To the Speaking Wall.

Otherwise, one speaks like this.

As I am speaking to you now.

9

Plain, uninspired, nothing of beauty about it.

Hearing Mr. U. coming down the hall, we wonder: Might tonight be Company?

But no. Soon, we find, it is mere Rehearsal. Mr. U.'s intention: to jam.

"Ted, where are you, what are you doing?" Mrs. U. inquires in the angry voice from elsewhere in the house.

"In the Listening Room," he says. "Jamming."

"Oh, for Lord's sake," she says.

It is a special feeling one gets when Mr. U. has sent your Pulse but it has not fully arrived. Like a pre-dreaming or déjà vu is how Craig and Lauren and I have described it on those rare occasions when, risking Penalty, we have spoken among ourselves. Once the Pulse is fully upon you, here will come your words, not intended by, but nevertheless flowing through, you, built, as it were, upon the foundation that is you, supercharged by the Pulse, molded to the chosen Topic, such that, if Mr. U. has dialed in, say, Nautical, whoever he has chosen to go first will suddenly begin Speaking of things Nautical in his or her own flavor, but far more compellingly than he or she could if unPinioned. Mr. U., jamming, may choose to have all of us Speak of Nautical simultaneously; in a whisper or quite loud; may Pan right to left (from Craig to Lauren to me, per our current Arrangement), each of us, in turn, putting his or her own spin on Nautical.

Tonight I feel the pre-dreaming/déjà vu feeling and then, *Across the slick vast field of the main deck aslant with the latest breaker,* I find myself calling out, *amid a positive Babel of shouted voices in manifold accents and dialects, hoary hands grip and release rain-slick masts as the rain pounds crosswise the darkwood deck veined by ancient ropes greenish with mold beneath the booted feet racing to address a faltering knot or stay as each lad wonders will he live out the storm or come to claustrophobic choking end sinking deep to expire in the watery Jones locker with the many-tentacled abyss creatures of the —*

Even as I am Speaking, I am aware of looks of pity, of commiseration, from Craig and Lauren, looks that seem to say: Although we are not exactly following you, good job, Jeremy, well Spoken, you are clearly doing your best to Speak of Nautical, and if the result is somewhat vague and hard to parse, well, that is the fault of Mr. U., who apparently has set your Prolixity too high.

But they dare not judge me too harshly.
For soon their Pulses too will come.

On Break we stay Pinioned, resting. Our current Pose: arms and legs thrown out wide, in the shape of the letter X, each of us askew at a slightly different angle.

Like stars, or a trio of folks falling from a great height.

Mr. U. comes back in with a beer and some chips.

"I think," he says, "City. A cityscape. What do you think?"

The Penalty for speaking being perpetually in effect, we merely nod, indicating: Sure, yes, City sounds good.

The Control Board allows Mr. U. to produce many shadings of Speech. It is not just City of which I (again first, I happily note) now begin Speaking; it is City, plus Sad, plus Summer; a dominant coloration of green-blue; City arranged N/S along a wide river. I am made to Speak in short, brisk sentences. Lauren, following me, Speaks, also, of a N/S-trending, river-spanning City, but, plus: Hunger, Raining, Exaltation, her whole Pass consisting of one long sentence. Craig is: City arranged E/W, white, Winter, no river, overrun by cats, alternating short and long sentences, and toward the end of his Pass, he begins to rhyme, or trying to rhyme, and is also Speaking, or attempting to Speak — Mr. U. is attempting to get him to Speak — in iambic pentameter (!).

For Finale, all three of us Speak of our Cities at once, as Mr. U. dials in Crescendo, such that afterward all three of our throats really hurt, so energetically does Mr. U. have us Speaking there at the end.

Mr. U. has been Recording. He plays us a snippet. Is pleased. So, we are pleased. Who would not be pleased? Well, Mrs. U. He calls her in, plays her the snippet.

"That is just some random noise, Ted," she says, and walks out.

We watch Mr. U. closely. Is he peeved? Seems to be. Yet still believes in us. We can tell by his smile, which says: Has she ever liked a piece of ours yet?

And we smile back: Not yet.

Mr. U. climbs the stepladder to pop into each of our mouths a lozenge. Jean, the maid, comes in with three water sponges on sticks, with which she moistens our lips, and then it is Dinner, and she Feeds us by attaching our Personal Feed Tubes to the tri-headed Master Feed Tube coming out of her large jar of Dining Mélange.

Then steps aside to read her book as we Dine.

Though sore-throated, we have elation: Interim is over.

Again we feel useful, creative, part of a team.

Late in the night the door creaks. Mrs. U. enters in nightwear. She steps directly to me, as always.

"Jeremy," she whispers. "Are you awake? I don't mean to bother. But."

"I'm awake," I whisper.

She wheels over Podium slowly, so as to maintain quiet, sets it just so. She slides a mic on a stand to my lips and dons headphones so as not to disturb the others or alert Mr. U. Sitting on the floor before me, she reaches behind and above herself to hit, on the Control Board, Go.

Tonight it is Rural, plus Ancient; overtones of Escape.

I begin Speaking (or, rather, per her Settings, Whispering, into the mic): of her Beauty, and we meet beside a placid Italian lake; in simple, objective sentences, for we are farmers; of the distant hills into which one day, I promise her, we will disappear; more of her Beauty; with quite high Specificity, and I find that, as I describe her

14

Beauty (her hips, her breasts, the way her hair falls across her shoulders in the early morning light, the way it makes me feel to glimpse her across the community table on feast days) I am becoming aroused, as is she, but also, if I may say it this way, am becoming, as well, in love with her, as, I believe, she is becoming in love with me, even though her family, her farming family, does not wish it, because she is betrothed to a cocksure troll of a man, son of the richest family in town, and as we pass hand in hand through a flock of sheep belonging to his family, which also owns the distant mill, she leans into me, indicating (I am Whispering all of this into the mic): I do not want him or his sheep, only you.

One new Feature tonight: a storm approaches. Soon we are drenched and I take off my outer garment and drape it across her slender shoulders. The storm is hers; it is in her Settings, part of Rural. But the garment-draping is mine; I supply that and can see that it pleases her, real her, sitting cross-legged there before me.

Then, beneath a waterfall, or actually just to one side of it, we make love, and I describe it well, and though I am Pinioned and therefore may not reach myself, Mrs. U. is not Pinioned, and may, and does,

15

reach herself.

As is often the case, I wonder whether it might not occur to Mrs. U., once she has been in that way unburdened, to stand up, step over, unburden me.

But it does not. It does not seem to occur to her. It never does. Never has yet.

Which is, I always feel, once my arousal has receded, probably for the best.

She merely rises to her feet abruptly, takes off the headphones, and, as if regretful, sharply wheels Control Podium back to where it was, restores the Dials to where they were, steps over to Lauren, then Craig, shining cellphone dimly upon them to see if they were awake during what just transpired. As usual, she concludes they were not. Sometimes, they really were not. (Paradoxically, though Pinioned and motionless all day, we are always exhausted at night.) On occasions when they have, in fact, been awake, as she approached with cellphone, they have quickly pretended to be asleep, not wanting her to feel in the least troubled.

All these four years she has never once gone to sit before Craig. Only me. And lately has begun sitting before me more often, and longer, to the extent that sometimes the dim harbinger of dawn, a sliver of yellow light that creeps in from what we believe was formerly a window but is now boarded up but not all that well, will fall across her lap, and she will leap to her feet, mumbling, for example, "What the hell, morning already?"

She is, that is, I believe, falling for me. And I am falling for her. When I first began Speaking to her of her Beauty it was, yes, mostly the Settings. The Settings said: Jeremy, Speak, while looking at me, of my Beauty. Also, my Specificity was always set, by her, to high. Speaking of her Beauty so often, with such high Specificity, made her Beauty real to me; made me notice it. (She really is so Beautiful.) As I began Speaking to her of her Beauty with more fervor (feeling more fervor, because noticing her Beauty with more Specificity, thereby Speaking of it with greater precision), she began, from there on the floor, to get, more and more often, a certain soft look upon her face, an arousal look, yes, but also a love look. I believe so.

She rarely speaks to me. I do not know her heart. Does she have love for me? When I am not Speaking to her? When she is, for example, elsewhere in the house, lost in her thoughts, having her day?

I can't know.

But I do know that never in my life have I

17

felt anyone to be as surpassingly Beautiful as I feel Mrs. U. to be when, Pulsed, I am Speaking with high Specificity of her Beauty and she is gazing up at me, looking for all the world as if she may love me.

Does that feeling pass? It does.

But also, it sort of endures.

That is: these days, I think of her constantly, and feel that I love her even when I am not Speaking to, or of, her, and she is nowhere near.

This morning Mr. U. leans in.

"Company tonight," he says. "We'll do City."

So: a long, anxious day. We would really like to Rehearse. But Mr. U. must go to Work. What I do to prepare: think about City, all day. Once we begin, it is mostly us. Our Speaking is being supercharged and made more articulate via the Pulse, yes, shaped, of course, by the Settings, but still, at the end of the day, it is, mostly, us. It is me, Craig, and Lauren, and we do not Speak identically well, if I may say so, and preparation is part (but only part) of the reason why one of us may, for example, tend to Speak better (in a more lofty, engaging way) than the others. There is also something innate: talent, one might term it.

It is not a competition. And yet it is.

What I have found: the more I live, in my mind, beforehand, within my Topic, the better my flow will be once I begin.

Mr. U. calls it: "priming the pump."

All day I prime my pump, getting to know my City better by thinking about it.

It is a Sad city, yes, for that is in the Settings, but I imagine a livelier quarter of the City, where all the City's celebration occurs, over there on a small island that may only be reached via canoe (a small fleet waits at a common pier).

What color are the canoes? Have they drivers? What is the direction of the current, as the drivers propel their canoes across the bay to the isle of celebration? Are there fireworks, which light up the faces of the shopkeepers and workers who have scrimped and saved to celebrate there, so that they may, for at least this one night, leave their sadness behind? The fireworks must, I imagine, be reflected, rippling, in the shallow water lapping in the narrow inlets that punctuate the island, along which orange-brown cafés are nestled, strung with tiny lights, lights that bob with any slight breeze, there in the cafés that nightly ring with the sound of the laughter of those relieved to find themselves made briefly joyful.

19

In this way, all day, while Lauren and Craig nap, I prime my pump.

Lauren wakes, gives me a look, as in: Jeremy, wait, are you priming your pump?

My look in return says: I am. Is that an issue?

Lauren and Craig feel that I am strange, too sensitive. I fall under the sway of the Settings, it is true, with greater alacrity than they. Always have. Well, I love my work. I aspire to always be feeling more, thus Speaking with more gusto, thus evoking greater emotion and engagement in my Listeners.

This is what, I feel, makes me unique among the three of us.

Around five Mr. U. comes home from Work. Still in Work suit, he steps into Listening Room and announces an inspiration, had at Work, for a new Arrangement: me, far left, ten feet above floor; Lauren in the middle, twenty feet above floor; Craig, far right, thirty feet above floor. We will thus make an ascending three-pointed line. We will be given, also, a new Pose, more in keeping with City: each of us standing upright, hands shading our eyes, as if gazing off at the distant Cities of which we will soon be Speaking.

Jed Dillon arrives to administer the Required Inter-Pose Stretching. Or, as he says it, "for to Stretch y'all."

Stretching, after nine days in the shape of the letter X, feels, as one might imagine, both good and bad.

We are then costumed in the mode of City dwellers: tuxedos for Craig and me, long flowing gown for Lauren.

Adult son Mike brings in a ladder, scaffolding, and the rubber-matted platforms upon which we must stand for re-Pinioning. Once in position, each of us leans his or her head back into the Fahey Cup, allowing the three Fahey pronglets to settle gently into the Fahey receptors at the base of the neck.

Then a test is run: Mr. U. makes each of us say the alphabet extremely fast, then extremely slow.

And we are ready.

We wait nervously, hearing the hum of Company as they enjoy Buffet in Main Living Area.

In they glide, smiling up at us politely, then take their seats in folding chairs grumpily put out earlier by adult son Mike. Mr. U. enters briskly in the blazer he dons for Performances, takes up his position at Podium. Mrs. U. takes up her position at rear of room, looking, if I may say so, pained, as if she wishes she could incur Penalty, then be forced to go sit in Penalty shed until Performance is done.

But alas: they are married, she must stay.

We begin.

Lauren goes first, Speaking of her City (arranged N/S along river, Hunger, Raining, Exaltation) in one long sentence. Midway through, Craig joins in, Speaking of his City in iambic pentameter: arranged E/W, no river, white, Winter, overrun by cats. Then, with Lauren and Craig still Speaking, I join, and Speak of my City (Sad, Summer, green-blue, arranged N/S along river, blue-green canoes oriented toward the celebration island like magnet needles, the lucky shopkeepers and workers dreamily trailing their hands behind in the cool, clean water, as, with fireworks bursting overhead, they are rowed past the orange-brown cafés toward the one bastion of happiness in their disappointing lives).

I feel I Speak beautifully of my City; I represent it well. Craig and Lauren also Speak well. Well enough. It is as if we are creating, for Company, those three Cities, upon those distant plains, while gazing out at what we have created, hands shading our eyes.

Even as we make our Cities, however, we

sense that Company is not thrilled. They gaze down at their feet, pretend to be reading the programs printed up by adult son Mike earlier in his room. Some yawn, others glance at the ceiling, as if longing to escape up through it. Wives elbow husbands, as in: Don't whisper that sarcastic comment to me just now, Ronald, I do not wish to be rude, by cracking up. When members of Company glance back at Mrs. U., she only lifts up her hands, as in: Honestly, I have no idea.

Mr. U., too, knows we are not killing it. In vain, with a red face, he desperately fine-tunes our Settings, positively sweating through Performance blazer.

Afterward, looking like he might cry, he accepts a series of false, contrived congrats from Company, then retreats with them into Main Living Area, for cake.

In Listening Room it is just me, Craig, Lauren, and the folding chairs, many of which have been knocked out of their rows by the haste in which Company fled.

Mr. U. rushes back in, tie loosened.

"Not your fault," he says. "You did everything I asked of you. I blame myself. We're going to think about this. Then try something new."

Our hearts go out to him. He works so

hard. And is always disappointed.

Then he sends in cake, which Jean holds up to our mouths on her Proffering Plate, at the end of her Reaching Rod, and on the sponges tonight there is wine, and the Feed feels richer than usual, as if Mr. U. has had some beef broth supplement put in there.

Craig and Lauren and I exchange mutual looks of: Goodness, what a trial.

Then, still standing upright, still dressed fancy, hands still shading our eyes, we sleep.

In the night, adult son Mike barges loudly in.

"Gosh, sorry," he says. "Did I wake you folks? Anything you need? I felt, honestly, so bad for you all tonight. That was the worst."

We would like to reply: Yes, adult son Mike, we know it was the worst. What we need now is sleep. Please go out.

But if we reply, adult son Mike may impose Penalty. He has done so before: imposed Penalty when we replied to a question he had just asked, which he would then claim was rhetorical.

Adult son Mike is a person of low character. It is best, we have found, not to engage with him.

Hence we merely stare ahead implacably.

"I just want you all to know," he says. "You're not alone. There are many of us who see this thing for the monstrous excess it is. You're human beings. You are. Even if the world — even if my parents — seem to have forgotten it. But help is coming. It is. Soon."

Then does his palms-together bow and leaves.

Lauren and Craig and I exchange looks of: Wow, thanks, adult son Mike, we did not know, until you just now told us, that we are human beings.

Then exchange worried looks.

It is always regrettable to have attracted the attention of adult son Mike.

We well remember the time when, having learned in grad school that costuming is one of the most fundamental and ancient modes of human self-expression, he demanded of Mr. and Mrs. U. that more attention be paid to our mode of dress. Adult son Mike can be quite the effective repetitive pain. He just never lets up. Soon, here came many pairs of slacks and various tunics and jean jackets and colorful hats, laid out before us on the floor of Listening Room, and each of us had to select those articles he or she found most appealing. Thereafter, our clothes were to be changed, by order of adult son Mike,

25

three times a day. And there went our downtime. It seemed we were just always having our clothes changed, by Jean. When Jean complained of overwork, Mr. and Mrs. U. pulled an intelligent fast one, by mandating that adult son Mike assist Jean. Adult son Mike, being a person of low character, unfond of work, made observably uncomfortable when forced to deal with the underwear of the males among us, i.e., Craig and me, soon withdrew his protest re costuming. And things returned to normal, i.e., we would wear Sweatsuit #1 for four days, after which Jean would change us into Sweatsuit #2 and take Sweatsuit #1 away to wash it.

And thus we got our downtime back.

Ever since, not a peep re costuming from adult son Mike.

So, tonight we worry. What did he mean, "help is coming"?

From where? For what? Why would help be needed here, where we all get along nicely and, with the exception of adult son Mike, have creative, fulfilling work to do?

Next morning brings a mood of defeat. Mr. U. comes in at nine. With a tray of Danishes. He seems to want to give us each a Danish of apology, but we are too high on the wall for him to reach. So, he sets the Danishes on a folding chair for now. In truth, none of us will ever get his or her Danish. They will just sit on that folding chair all day.

Because what a day it turns out to be.

"I hope you will forgive me for the debacle that was last night," Mr. U. says. "Today is about a new start. And making amends. Sometimes, in art, in life, one has to invest. Whether one's wife approves or not. If and when she finds out."

Then gulps nervously. As if for comic effect. And yet not.

How we love Mr. U.

Jed Dillon and Jean come in. Our City clothes are removed, by Jean, who then assists us in redonning Sweatsuits #1. We Stretch, are put into a new Pose (standing erect, hands hanging free) in a new Arrangement: standing on floor, very close to one another, Craig tight against the wall, then Lauren, then me. It is the closest to each other we have ever stood. Won't this look errant? we wonder. To Company? A gloriously wide, tall Speaking Wall, and three Speakers huddled in one corner, as if Listening Room had tilted in the night and all had slid over?

Mr. U. disappears behind the Speaking

Wall to reposition our Anterior Receptors.

"You may be wondering what's going on," he says from back there.

We are.

"Jed!" he calls out.

At which, Jed leads in eleven Singers. We know they are Singers by their vests. The first comes over, stands next to me, his arm against mine, as the others fill in along the length of the wall.

Then Mr. U. comes back out, holding aloft a small box.

"Anybody know what this guy is?" he says.

We do know, courtesy of fallen Ed, our colleague, briefly with us, then sent away for spreading lies.

It is: Knowledge Mod.

We know it by its bright red casing.

Gosh, we feel, Mr. U. is not joking around, Knowledge Mods being, per fallen Ed, not cheap.

Mr. U. spends the next ten minutes on his side, shirt hiked up, grunting, swearing, wiring the Mod into the Control Board.

Then it is time to try.

The Pulse from a Knowledge Mod, we find, is fatter, with stinging edge, a bit of a spiky pillow. It opens out nicely on the back end, like a forced jig-dancing at the end of a long and tedious day.

And suddenly we know so much. About "Battle of the Little Bighorn." Also known as "Custer's Fight." Or, popularly, "Custer's Last Stand." None of which, I can tell you, previous to right now, I knew.

"Name of horse Custer rode into battle?" Mr. U. says, testing.

"Vic," we three Speakers say at once.

"Although Dandy was also along," says Craig.

"And many incorrectly believe it was Comanche," says Lauren, "which was the name of the sole surviving Seventh Cavalry horse."

"Who was actually ridden into battle by Captain Myles Keogh," I add, smiling at how pleasant it is to suddenly know all of this.

"What tribes, peacefully gathered in the valley of the Little Bighorn, did Custer and his men attack?" says Mr. U.

"Lakota, Arapaho, Northern Cheyenne," says Lauren.

"Members of which tribe, the historical enemies of the Lakota, served as scouts for Custer?" says Mr. U.

"Crow, also known as Absaroka," we all say at once.

The Singers, who cannot Speak, or even talk, just nod, as if to say: Though we, as

29

part of our development, have been rendered mute unless Pulsed and Singing, we agree with all that has just been Spoken by our colleagues.

Mr. U. claps his hands once, hard, as if pleased.

"This will be great," he says, then goes to Lunch.

The Singers emit a prolonged one-note group hum, the women an octave above the men, which we understand to mean: Hi, hello, looking forward to working with you all on what promises to be a truly exciting and original project.

Being on a Knowledge Mod is, let us say, different.

It is not just us emptily riffing, as usual, on general concepts such as Nautical, such as City. Now we are given facts. Real facts. Which are helpful. In making compelling structure. It is like walking down a tight hallway, constrained on either side by gray walls of fact. It is like stumbling through a desert and suddenly a mist of knowledge rains down composed of the exact details you have been craving but did not previously know you craved.

Mr. U. unfolds the Timeline Chart that came with the Mod, binder-clips it across two music stands. Turns out, he is a whiz at Shaping: at Shaping who Speaks what facts, for how long, and in what order.

What results is like a story.

And even we are more interested.

I am Private Fritz Neubauer, frightened German immigrant, who joined the Seventh Cavalry because I could find no other gainful employment. My boots are the wrong size, and they hurt. My English is poor. I am not sure how to properly load my weapon. Craig is Yellow Dog, a young Lakota teased by his fellows for his good looks, swimming in the Little Bighorn, having stayed up too late dancing last night, making many new friends among the gathered tribes. He has chosen this portion of the river because, just there, beneath the cottonwoods, some young women, Black Leg Doe among them, are gathering wild turnips. She is over there now, frowning, pretending to scour the ground near the far bank, so that Yellow Dog may see her and she may, as she now does, look up, see him, feign surprise, then smile, admitting, by that smile, that her surprise was feigned. They look frankly at each other for a few seconds, after which she turns to rejoin her friends, knowing he is watching her go. Everyone is happy. It is a glorious summer morning, with nothing to be done for the rest of the day.

Lauren is Major Marcus Reno, ordered by Custer to take his battalion and attack the village at its south end. Custer has promised to support him in this. Reno would prefer to stay with the main group. He has never been in a proper Indian fight. But off he rides. When the village comes into sight, the battalion breaks into a gallop. The men whoop. Soon they will be covered in glory. In the distance: white shapes, fragile structures, containing human beings. The aim is to fire into the tents, ride over them, cause a panic, chase down and kill any who flee on foot.

But now a dozen or so Hunkpapas appear, riding back and forth in the path of the advance, raising dust in an attempt to gain the women and children time to escape.

Structured by facts, we feel a sense of urgency. This really happened, is really happening. How will it turn out? Will Private Neubauer live through the coming fight? Will Yellow Dog? Will Black Leg Doe? Are there not children in the village? What will become of them? Why are these mounted men so bent on attacking this peaceful gathering? We honestly do not know. Either Mr. U. has loaded only part of the Mod, or the Mod itself possesses a tight temporal confinement feature, i.e., reveals itself only gradually, i.e., is arranged into "chapters." In any event, we are, so to speak, on the edge of our seats. We are still riffing somewhat on top of the facts (I have, for example, given the private a riding-related back injury not suggested by the Mod), but with so many facts at our disposal, there is less need, as well as less room within which, to riff.

Then our Singers join in.

And it is a wonderment.

Sometimes they will double, with their Singing, the words we are Speaking. Other times they arrange themselves into two- or three-Singer clusters, Singing the experiences of individuals peripheral to the main action (those proximate to Private Neubauer, Reno, Yellow Dog, or Black Leg Doe, for example). At one point, each Singer becomes a different Lakota youth racing along the banks of the river, back toward the village, sounding the alarm. In a truly startling moment, all eleven Singers break into a complex fugue representing the collective mindstate of Reno's troops as they attack (their excitement, their longing for home, their anticipation of a quick, painless victory).

33

Even as we are part of it, are somewhat lost in it, we know it is amazing.

Mr. U. puts us on Pause.

"My gosh," he says. "My goodness."

We Speakers, we Singers stand there, out of breath, proud and beautiful in our exhaustion.

Like the horses of the Seventh, we think, like the ponies of the tribes.

We Rehearse late into the night, running through it again and again, adding layers of detail with each Pass.

Warriors on horseback begin appearing on Reno's flanks. He has been drinking whiskey from a flask all morning. Stricken by anxiety, fearing an ambush, he halts the charge, orders the men into a skirmish line. With this, all hope of a quick victory is lost. Hundreds of warriors materialize, as if from the dust. Among Reno's troopers, order begins to break down. Men sneak away from the line, taking refuge in a grove of trees nearby. In the grove, Reno's Arikara scout, Bloody Knife, is shot in the head. His brains splatter across Reno's face. This traumatic event (marked by the Singers with a series of jarring, atonal chords) unhinges Reno. He calls for his men to dismount, then remount. Abruptly, he bolts away ahead of his troops without sounding the retreat. Later he will claim this was meant to be a charge through the Indian lines. In fact, badly frightened, he has forgotten entirely about his men, these men who have entrusted him with their lives. Many die now, ridden down like buffalo by warriors as they try to reach, and then cross, the river. Some who have lost their horses are killed as they scramble on hands and knees up what will evermore be known as Reno Hill.

Having incurred grave losses, the battalion, or what remains of it, is now gathered atop this hill, surrounded, dispirited, disoriented, under siege.

Where is Custer? we Speak, we Sing.

We Speakers ask this in a range of American accents being supplied to us by the Mod. The Singers ask this repeatedly, in a melody (the Mod somehow tells us even this) adapted from the main theme of an obscure Italian opera by a composer named Federici.

But there is no answer, no one knows where Custer is; he was last seen an hour ago, on the ridge above, as we embarked upon our ill-fated attack, waving his hat to us, believing us soon to be victorious, riding off to the north with the several companies

35

in his charge.

We wait on Reno Hill all afternoon, in the great heat, desperate for water, being fired upon whenever we move, expecting at any moment to be overrun by these powerful fiends who, having so mastered us, now seem an utterly supernatural force, beyond our power to resist.

And then we become those "fiends," those Lakota, Arapaho, and Northern Cheyenne, these sons and husbands and brothers, to whom the white devils on the hill no longer appear frightening (as they did in the early moments of the attack, when the sleepy village was caught by surprise) but, instead, pitiful and disgusting; they have traveled far, to kill our children, and when we fought back like men, they panicked, threw down their arms, cried, begged, crawled away.

From all across the village, we begin streaming south to confront them.

We hope we will succeed in killing them all before night.

Mr. U. abruptly shuts us down.

It is a bit of a shock, to be merely ourselves again.

"You are making me very happy," Mr. U. says.

I raise my hand.

Mr. U. points at me, indicating that I may

36

speak without fear of Penalty.

"How long ago was all of this?" I say.

Mr. U. seems pleased to have been asked.

"Well, what we've covered so far?" he says. "Took place on June twenty-fifth, 1876."

"When is it now?" I say.

He smiles, shakes his head, gives a little laugh.

"I'd say it's time for some sleep," he says.

Mr. U. turns off the lights, exits Listening Room.

What we know, what we retain of what we just now knew, floats about in our heads like the dust we made as we rode. In dreams that soon come, we are Lakota, Arapaho, whites, Cheyenne, Crow, moving freely about a room-sized scale model of the battlefield, shouting jokes, racing our mounts, suddenly friends, having forgotten entirely that just now, in the daylight, we desired to obliterate one another.

I wake in the night to find Mrs. U. wheeling over Podium. She slides the mic stand over, Sets her Settings, dons the headphones, sits, leans back.

We are still on the Mod, the Mod she does not yet know Mr. U. has purchased, which, when she reaches behind and above herself to hit Go, Auto-Engages me at a random

37

Location within itself, overriding whatever Settings she has just now Set.

I find myself Whispering to her in the form of a letter from a captain, a Captain Evers of Minnesota, longing for her, his wife, even as he, on his belly, waits for Reno Hill to be overrun. Nearby, friends of his, dear to him from many years of service, weep in terror. The body of Carvelli lies where he fell, shot between the eyes as he deliriously sought water. None of us has ever been this thirsty. We experience this thirst as a kind of madness. From somewhere a woman is shrieking. It is not a woman. It is Dietzen, the trumpeter. Our enemies seem able to instantly kill whoever does not lie flat, mouth full of the dry earth. Someone tells Dietzen to be quiet; someone remonstrates with him to show some pride. Dietzen goes on shrieking.

How did we, the mighty Seventh, come to this? We are aghast to have been so reduced by what we had imagined to be a paltry force of feeble savages but turned out to be a swift killing machine perfectly pitched to existing conditions of geography and landscape. We wish to go home, start over, never have come here.

Now, for the error of coming, we must die here, by hand, as it were: war-clubbed, pierced through with arrows, shot or knifed at close range. We have, mere hours ago, seen certain dear friends of ours perish in precisely these ways.

It will happen. It will happen soon.

It will happen soon, to me, I fear. To this precious body, which I have known and loved all my life.

I mention none of this in my letter. To my wife. She is delicate. It is not, anyway, a real letter, for I have nothing with which to write and no light by which to see; I write her this letter in my mind, to give myself comfort. Though things are dire, I tell her (I Whisper, to Mrs. U.), I am taking comfort in a certain memory of her that, in other circumstances, I would be hesitant to mention but that, tonight, it seems neglectful not to recall with the deepest gratitude: her, kneeling upon our bed, the Christmas Eve of the first year of our marriage, wearing the robe I brought back west for her from Cleveland, wind howling outside, and yet there in our home all was close and warm.

And then, I write (I Whisper), you were generous enough to allow that garment to fall away, and in the firelight I beheld a sight that inspired in me a feeling of awe the likes of which no western vista could ever hope to rival.

During all of this, Mrs. U. makes no move to unburden herself but is only training upon me the most rapt attention.

Which emboldens me somewhat.

Every man (I Whisper) is born with a certain store of desire. It is a treasure he has been bequeathed, that he must spend wisely over the course of his life. One moves through the world, finding objects on which to expend it. Blessed is he who finds a worthy object, shaped by God, provided fortuitously unto him, that elicits his longing so strongly that all else briefly recedes and he becomes pure desire. Then, wonder of wonders: that which he desires, embodied, may become pure desire herself, desiring him. Here is what I wish to say, dearest one, trapped as I am on this desolate, godless hillside, surrounded by demons who wish to destroy me: because I have known such a moment with you (the firelight playing across the walls; the dog asleep against the door; the bed shifting beneath us, as if making approving commentary in its own unique language), I may die now, if I must die, knowing I have truly lived.

Mrs. U. stands, approaches, drops her bathrobe.

Is naked before me.

"Praise me," she whispers.

I do.

I do so.

I praise her. Her legs, hips, waist, breasts, neck, hair, eyes. I praise it all. I am not a captain from Minnesota, I say. I am me, I am Jeremy, one of your Speakers. And I adore you. She blinks twice, startled, but does not look away. I tell her that, Pinioned here, I am able, by a process of listening with focused attention, to know, at any given time, what portion of Main Living Area she is occupying and what she is doing there; that is, in what work she is engaged. She does so much for the household. She is always improving something, arranging something, putting into play something that will cause life to be easier and better for Mr. U. and adult son Mike. Their lives are made better by her, through her care, though they seem oblivious to, and only rarely acknowledge, this. I want her to know that I, who have had ample time (four years, two months) to objectively observe her, find her wonderful, glorious, thoroughly lovable.

When I have finished, she steps forward, kisses me.

"I'm so lonely here," she says.

"I know," I say, risking Penalty.

She kisses me again, with more push, more lingering, a slight motion of biting.

41

There comes a sound from Main Living Area.

She redons her bathrobe, rearranges Podium, shuts all down, goes swiftly away.

Craig emits a long, low whistle.

Lauren makes a *tsk-tsk* sound.

The Singers emit a series of quick chromatic bursts, as if to inquire: Gosh, in what sort of home do we find ourselves?

But I can hardly sleep for the joy of it all.

It is, yes, of course, complicated. I love Mr. U. Is this not a betrayal of his trust? It is, I know it is. I do not wish to disturb the happiness of our family. I have known these dear people all my life.

And yet.

Mrs. U., also a member of the family, desires, even needs, these evenings with me.

And I (another member of the family) also desire and need them, truth be told.

The world in which I have received a biting kiss from the beautiful Mrs. U. is a better world than the one in which I have not. I refuse — or, rather, decline — to act in such a way as to preclude further such biting kisses, to preclude the possibility that, some night not long from now, she may, moved by further risks I intend to take in my Speaking, allow me to (sweet thought)

42

touch her, with my hands (should my operative Pose, at that time, leave my hands un-Pinioned), and even to kiss other parts of her, or the possibility that she may (Good God) do certain bold things to me, with her hands, with her mouth, things that I know about, although, to be honest, I am not entirely sure how I know about them.

What is right, what is wrong? In this situation?

What a small question!

What is great? That is what my heart longs to ask. What is lush? What is bold, what is daring? In which direction lies maximum richness, abundance, delight?

This is all new to me, this wanting of something. I want further congress with her more than I want what I have previously always wanted most: i.e., to be so good at what I do that none may find fault with me and everyone is super pleased with me and agrees that I have no real competition in my field.

Might I still accomplish this goal while pursuing and winning the affections of Mrs. U.?

I believe so.

I hope so.

Theirs is, I know from close observation (it pains me to say this), a dead marriage. I, by being the new life that will begin coursing through Mrs. U., will, in a sense, save them both. Mr. U., seeing our fresh new love, will, so to speak, yield the field, and find renewed and focused pleasure in his work at Podium, discreetly leaving the nights to us. And, in time, he will come to love someone new, perhaps aided by Mrs. U. Perhaps it will be her friend Hazel, who sometimes drops by, or her other friend Sandra, who, in my eyes, is prettier and happier than Hazel, who, stepping into Listening Room, only tends to wince and step back out, who knows why.

So let it be Sandra.

I make a mental note to broach this topic with Mrs. U. during our next evening together.

We Rehearse for the next two days.

Then it is the day of the night of Performance.

At three, Jed comes in to Rearrange us. We Speakers, in standing postures, are formed into a tight triangle midway up the Speaking Wall, encircled by our Singers. One of our Singers, afraid of heights, reassured at length by the other Singers, must finally be given an Ativan, by Jean.

Since each of us will be Speaking/Singing

44

from multiple viewpoints, costuming is kept simple: each of us is to wear a new black Sweatsuit. Adult son Mike, grumbling, takes the plastic-wrapped Sweatsuits from the Target box, one by one, and lays them out on the floor of Listening Room, so that he and Jean may check sizes, see who gets what.

"What an event, what a night," he says.

"Mike," Jean says. "No sarcasm. We've got a lot to do."

"A bunch of old rich people get to hear an old rich guy tell the story of a bunch of youngish imperialist oppressors dying gloriously," says adult son Mike. "Performed by a group of people who, unbeknownst to themselves, are currently being oppressed by the old guy and his rich pals in the audience, who he insists on boring to death every few weeks and who consent to it in the name of friendship and are thereby made complicit in the whole oppressive shit show."

"Does anyone in here look oppressed, Mikey?" Jean says. "Other than you? Look around."

We Speakers, regarding ourselves in our new black Sweatsuits, are smiling. The Singers, in their new black Sweatsuits, ditto. We are smiling because we like our look, yes, but also because we are in a state of high anticipation, because we have been working at something deep and complex and surprising that we are soon going to have the chance to gift to a group of people not at all expecting to be wowed.

A feeling adult son Mike has, sadly, never known.

He has no work, no art, no dreams, no joy. He just has anger and a fondness for being correct in his energetic, self-righteous disapproval of all that he sees.

He comes over, stands before us.

"Jeremy, what are you?" he says. "Like, thirty?"

I give him a look, as in: Funny, adult son Mike.

"No, seriously," he says. "How old are you?"

I raise my hand.

"Go," he says.

"Four," I say.

"Right, you're four," he says. "Four years old."

"And two months," I say.

Lauren and Craig nod, as in: We are also four years, two months.

"Pretty big for four-year-olds," he says. "Plus, Craig, your hair is thinning."

Craig blushes, casts sad eyes up in the direction of his hair.

"Mike, honestly," says Jean. "You need to grow up, show some respect. For your dad's work."

Jean must have been a maid here a long time for adult son Mike, normally so peevish and combative, to shrug off this rebuke.

"So, you were all born, like, full-sized, on the same day, four years ago?" he says. "That was, it seems to you, your, uh, birthday? Your collective birthday?"

I nod, Lauren smiles, Craig gives a thumbs-up, meaning: As far as we are aware, that is correct.

"Who were your mothers?" he says. "Have you ever considered that?"

We have. We have even quietly spoken of it. One of our earliest shared memories is of being told, by Jean, that our respective mothers gave birth to us here but then had to go, as our moms had other babies to give birth to, elsewhere. Our moms were quite busy giving birth to Speakers all over the land, Jean explained, doing a real service for the world by filling it with advanced-level Speakers. Because of our moms, many people were going to experience so much pleasure, in Listening Rooms from coast to coast.

It was a long explanation, so long it had to be read from a laminated card, and something about having to read it put Jean in a soft mood, and she never did get to the end of it but soon dropped the card in the trash and used her Reaching Rod to offer us a series of sweet treats, which is when we first started to feel that we were really going to like it here.

And we have. We really have liked it here.

"But where were you before you came here?" says adult son Mike.

"I'm going to go get your dad," Jean says.

"Go ahead," says adult son Mike. "He knows where I stand on this crap."

Jean goes.

"Heaven," I say.

"Heaven, okay," says adult son Mike. "Let's go with that. Then what? You dropped, fully grown, out of your mom's vagina? Moms' vaginas? Think about it, guys. How big a woman would these ladies have to be for that shit to work out? I mean, do the math."

Mr. U. comes in.

"I thought we'd agreed that this wasn't happening anymore," he says.

"Fine, Dad," adult son Mike says. "Have fun with your 'show.' Have fun choreographing your reactionary History Channel bullshit. Which, by the way, seems to be badly neglecting the Indigenous perspective. But don't blame me. Don't blame me for any of it."

"Michael, Mikey," Mr. U. says. "You're misunderstanding. It was a signal event in history. The American *Iliad,* if you will."

"Ugh, Jesus!" shouts adult son Mike.

Stomping out, he flicks the lights off, on, off.

Mr. U. follows adult son Mike out.

Jean goes over, flicks the lights back on.

"Forget him, guys," she says to us. "Just do your thing. Have fun."

We plan to. We plan to just do our thing, have fun.

In an hour or so, Mr. U. returns, bearing history books. Sitting cross-legged near the Mod, he laboriously hand-inputs much new material intended to address adult son Mike's critique re the paucity of Indigenous accounts. Once that is done, we must, of course, because we are pros, Rehearse, especially the new bits, so that all will be seamless, which takes the better part of the afternoon.

Company arrives at seven.

Fewer in number than before. As if word about our last Performance has gotten out.

But that is fine.

The fifteen or so gathered here are, we

know, in for something special.

Mrs. U. is, as usual, in the back row, looking chagrined in advance. I would like to catch her eye. But am in work mode. In my mind, I dedicate my Performance to her, hoping that something in it will captivate and impress her enough to draw her to me tonight, post-Performance.

I feel my chances are good.

For I have been given a major Solo.

Mr. U. taps Control Podium with his baton.

We begin.

Reno advances toward the village. The Lakota youths race along the river, crying out in alarm. I am again Private Neubauer, Craig again Yellow Dog, Lauren again Reno. The charge falters, the skirmish line is formed, the horse-holders, responsible for four nervous mounts each, quake in the shade of the box elder trees. Bloody Knife is shot, Reno panics, precedes his terrified men to the top of the hill. Unhorsed, out of ammunition, riven with fear, they follow, our Singers conveying their terror in dissonant counterpoint. Many troopers are killed along the way, as they cross the river or try to climb the steep cliff on its opposite side, bludgeoned with war club or hatchet or rifle butt.

On Reno Hill, the corpses begin to bloat in the withering heat. Reno is drunk, cantankerous, useless. We, his men, are terrified and confused. Some are ranting. Carvelli falls. Dietzen shrieks. Some of us begin to dig in. Rudimentary breastworks are constructed of packs and food tins. The horses are moved into a slight declension in the center of the defensive perimeter, where an ad hoc field hospital has been established.

Surrounded on the hill, all of us, Singers and Speakers alike, cry out for Custer. Why has he not come to support us, as promised?

There is no answer.

We last saw him up on the ridge, but he is not there now.

Abandoned, we reflect on he who, we believe, has abandoned us. To do so, we become him. Craig, Lauren, and I, respectively, are him as: a child, a brash West Point cadet, a Civil War hero/young suitor of Libbie, with whom he exchanges torrid, pornographic letters. Six of the Singers voice Custer at his most arrogant, five at his most insecure. We convey his anxious American ambition, his love of dogs, his manic, staccato way of speaking when excited, his erratic communications skills, his wild confidence in battle.

Then, moving down into the valley, as the

51

Singers provide a lush placeholding triad, we Rewind, go back in time, begin living out the morning from the collective mind-state of the village.

The day begins quietly. We feel happy and at peace. Yellow Dog flirts with Black Leg Doe. Shots ring out. In the early moments of the attack, Sitting Bull sends his nephew One Bull and the nephew's friend Good Bear Boy out toward Reno's men to broker a peace. Good Bear Boy is shot through both legs and One Bull heroically drags him back to camp, using a lariat. Sitting Bull's horse is shot out from under him. Abandoning thoughts of peace, he orders a counterattack. Too old to fight, he helps the women and children flee north to safety.

One of those riding out to meet Reno is Crazy Horse. Craig, Lauren, and I, respectively, voice him as: a precociously athletic child; a brash young lover who courted the wife of another man and was shot in the face for it; a mystic atop a hillside, seeking a vision without first undergoing the necessary purification rituals.

Six of the Singers voice Crazy Horse as a transcendent holy man (instructed, in that vision, to eschew all possessions and always ride into battle unadorned; loved not just for his bravery but for his abundant charity to the poor), five as a hermit, slightly mad. (Known within the community as "Our Strange Man," he continued to court Black Buffalo Woman, the wife of No Water, even after the birth of her third child, his version of courting being to linger near their lodge uninvited for days on end.)

Here he is now, thundering past, single feather in his hair, stone behind one ear, no paint on his body but for a few quick smears to represent lightning and snow, riding out to meet Reno.

Lauren becomes Red Deer Woman, whose son, Rabbit, was born with a withered leg; he is ten, too big to carry. Friends, aunties, mothers, toddlers flee past. Her mouth is dry with dust. Why have they come so far to kill us, to kill the likes of him, so gentle with everyone and everything, simple in that way (a protector of downed birds, a worrier over fallen buffalo)?

Her husband is Three Horn. He has gone with Crazy Horse to engage Reno. May he be safe. He is rash, proud, impulsive. One of the congenial rituals of their marriage is that, at night, she will drape her small, cold body over his large one and in this way warm herself. Must I always be your fire? he will say, a smile in his voice in the dark.

The boy is moving along well now. She

must be patient.

For the moment, all is quiet. There is no need to rush him.

He looks up, smiles apologetically; she ruffles his hair, and they move on.

Why must we be perpetually harassed by these literal, stupid killers? What is it that compels these disordered creatures to leave their own families behind and ride these many miles to attack us? They are humans in appearance, yet their minds seem to function not in human fashion but with the selfish shortsightedness of animals. They resemble pigs in their coloration and attitudes. These clothed pigs have come, mounted on horses, into the tender skeleton of the village, sputum in their unkempt beards, wild looks in their bloodshot eyes, as at the Washita (she was there; two of her brothers died there), where they took many women and children hostage, later making use of the women, some of whom have now drifted back, broken.

It is a good day to die, the warriors shout as they ride toward the white invaders, and they try to believe it, though their throats are dry and their hearts are pounding and the dear ones they may never see again are rapidly receding behind them; it is a good day to die, they shout, and must believe it, so that they will be able to do whatever is required of them in the terrible moments ahead, unimpeded by any longing to remain in this sweet, still-opening-to-them world.

I sneak a look at Mr. U. He is pure concentration. Are we doing well? We are. He knows it. He has them. He has Company. It is a different sort of sweat on him now: the sweat of a man bent on bringing a thing to glorious conclusion after many years of humiliation.

I sneak a look out at Company. Company is rapt. No one is examining their programs or longing to fly up through the ceiling. A wife gives her and her husband's conjoined hand a single shake, as in: Good, right? He gives a shake back: Yes, so glad we came.

Mrs. U., in the back row, is standing, as if at attention, as if something inside is urging her to take fresh notice of this man she has, all of these years, underestimated. He is, in Performance, manifesting an energetic verve, a focused attention that, one feels, he has, all these years, been denying her.

Adult son Mike appears in the doorway, steps out, then steps back in, as if waiting for someone to arrive.

Perhaps adult son Mike has invited a date? This would be good. Perhaps, to become nicer, all adult son Mike needs is a little companionship. After all, his parents are super nice.

And, of all the nights on which adult son Mike might have invited a date, this is the best.

Because we are absolutely killing it and everyone in here knows it.

A silence falls across the valley of the Little Bighorn. Reno's men, still pinned down, hear only the sound of their own shallow breathing. Around them, in ravines and washes, warriors move stealthily forward on hands and knees, watching for any movement from the hillside. They are young, many of them, and nervous, but this is a chance they have long dreamed of: the enemy is well and truly theirs.

Across the valley and to the north, Custer pauses on a promontory.

Before him is the largest Indian village he has ever seen.

He pauses to think.

So much depends on what he does next.

In a sort of interregnum, the Singers describe the deer, bobcats, elk, mountain lions that abound in the vicinity. They Sing the fluttering leaves of the aspen; the lapping of the creek as, ignorant of battle or non-battle, it moves as always among the rocks; the sound the wind makes as it crosses the plain, smoothly accommodating hillsides, washes, crags, ravines.

But the silence cannot hold.

The killing must soon begin again in earnest.

We Speakers and Singers, all at once, begin voicing the syllable *O,* in grief, in awe, in amazement at what is about to happen here, in the middle of nowhere, in this patch of dry grass and rolling hills that, had this army not come, would have remained unremarked by history, like innumerable similar places across the west, lost to history because no mass death occurred there.

Gathered on this summer afternoon, up on the ridges, below in the valley, are a specific number of living, breathing human beings whose fate it is to die today, some three hundred or so who woke this morning not imagining it would be their last.

Why? Why must this be? Is there not abundance enough and beauty to support all in peace, were that the general intention?

There is.

But peace is not the general intention. It is not the intention of the army. It is not the intention of the nation the army represents. The intention of the nation is to have this land for itself, uncontested.

57

The intention of the tribes is to continue to exist, here on land that, in truth, has changed hands many times before, often by violence, i.e., on land seized by force from other people. Members of the tribes have also set upon peaceful homes, abducted women, killed children.

Peace is not, apparently, the general human intention, although in the spare hour (in the dear home, in the individual heart) it may sometimes seem to be.

In any event, the thing has gone too far, and must now be brought to completion.

We know from Rehearsal how it will end: Custer, attempting to attack the north end of the village, will be driven back by the heroic actions of White Cow Bull, Roan Bear, White Shield, Bobtail Horse, Dull Knife, Buffalo Calf, and Mad Wolf, among others, who will, through the rapid, accurate firing of their Winchester and Henry repeating rifles, hidden in a low place among willows, seem to represent a larger force. The charge will falter; the attacking soldiers will be driven back the way they came. Thousands of warriors, converging from every direction, will encircle and descend upon the soldiers, who, as they struggle to find a place from which to fight, will die in distinct groups, some forming themselves into skirmish lines, others frightened into paralysis, losing all sense of reality. Some, fearing torture, will kill themselves (singly or in prearranged pairs). Others will fight on bravely to the end. Some, out of ammunition, will drop their weapons and flee madly, only to be swiftly run down by pursuing warriors on horseback.

Oh, John!, one trooper will call out to the mounted brave about to bash in his brains, using the name the troopers apply to all Indians.

Finally, there will remain only a small huddle of men, including Custer, on a slight rise that will forever bear the name Last Stand Hill.

And there they will die.

All of this will happen within the next forty minutes.

But none of it has happened yet.

Custer sits astride Vic, grasping the full extent of the village for the first time.

O, we Sing.

O, we Speak.

Where is Custer? cry the men on Reno Hill. We fear he has left us here to die.

Where is Custer? cries the village. We fear he has tricked us and will now destroy us from the north.

And this is where Mr. U. has decided

59

Intermission will be.

All Speaking stops, all Singing stops. As instructed by Mr. U., we go limp, stand motionless, hang our heads, there upon the Speaking Wall.

At Podium, Mr. U. also hangs his head. He does not need to turn to know what Company thinks. He knows. We know.

We know very well how powerful we have been.

Company rises to its feet, its wild enthusiasm seeming impatient that its only path into the world is via these limited, applauding, middle-aged bodies.

Mrs. U. moves up the aisle (dances up it, nearly), embraces Mr. U., kisses him, here in Listening Room, in front of Company.

I feel, I admit it, a twinge of jealousy.

And yet, it is good, seeing them happy together. It is. They are a family. They are our family. We are a family. It is good for all of us if they are happy.

On the other hand, if they are happy, how will I ever be? When my future happiness depends upon further biting kisses? I imagine the lonely nights to come, should they reconcile, as I hang bereft on the Speaking Wall, hearing their laughter, perhaps their lovemaking (!), emanating, perhaps, from the couch in Main Living Area, from which, long ago, just after my birth, in the days before their estrangement, I once heard those sounds coming, the little startled yips she made, which, even then, though I was only newly born, aroused me.

But then again: she is his wife, his oldest friend, his helpmate. This kiss may be merely a friendship kiss, to say: Dear, I am genuinely happy to see that you have not, once again, failed.

Mr. U. thinks to have Jean bring us water. As we are drinking, Company's applause redoubles, as if to say: Of course, yes, it is they who have done the work, my goodness, let them drink.

Company files out for Intermission, casting glances of admiration back at us.

But there is to be no Intermission for us: we have much to do, if we are to make Second Half surpass First.

Jed and Jean quickly bring out the ladder, the scaffolding, the rubber-matted platforms.

"Where's Mike?" Jed says. "He's supposed to be helping."

"Forget that little shit," says Jean. "He's been distracted all day."

The platforms are situated beneath us. We

61

are unPinioned and climb down the ladder one by one. We try to be swift without rushing. It will not do for us to be winded once we begin. The Singers are also unPinioned and climb down. Jed works his way along the row of us, gently inserting, into our Fahey receptors, the small wireless device called the RoamStar.

Equipped with the RoamStar, we no longer need to be attached to Listening Wall, but, feet and hands free, may now do our Speaking, our Singing, from anywhere at all.

A test is run: Jed has each of us Speakers wander around the Room while saying the alphabet extremely fast, then extremely slow.

Then the Singers are made, while wandering, to Sing major then minor scales, all the way up, all the way down.

We arrange ourselves along the front wall, heads leaning back, so that when Company returns, it will appear that our heads are, as before, nestled in our Fahey Cups. At the critical moment (as Custer reaches the small rise on which he will die, understanding, finally, that Reno's attack on the village has failed, that his forces are outnumbered by perhaps ten to one, that his famous luck has run out), we will (surprise, surprise) step away from the wall and, voicing the encroaching Lakota, Arapaho, and Cheyenne, surround Company, moving aggressively into them, out among them. This will increase the immediacy of their experience, make them feel, as Custer and his men must have felt, the impossibility of escape. Death is coming, coming soon, it is nearly upon them; it is upon them. Mr. U. has encouraged us, as we Speak and Sing, to touch Company, climb over them, make them feel our presence. We aim to discomfit, he says, to make them understand that this thing actually happened, it involved real people, people just like themselves.

Mr. U. leans in, sees that all is progressing well, gives us a thumbs-up, and several of us give him a convivial thumbs-up in return.

This is going to be so good.

We watch Company's faces as, returning from Intermission, they notice us standing on the floor, down from the Wall.

Mr. U. strides to Podium, visibly buoyed by the sincere praise he has received during Intermission.

He taps Podium once, crisply, with his baton.

We begin.

Custer attempts to attack the north end of

63

the village but is driven back by White Cow Bull et al. In the attempt, an officer, possibly Custer himself, is shot. The men are confused, paralyzed, by this unexpected event, the first death of the day among that wing of the Seventh. Thousands of warriors now bear down upon them. It is the beginning of the end. They are pursued back up the coulee, fighting well at first, though hampered by their need to bear along the wounded officer. Then it is happening fast, too fast, faster than any of them could have imagined. There is no time to think, reconsider, pray. A man — a boy, really — from Kansas stands aghast, watching four braves on horseback approach. He has lost his gun and his left boot. He wishes to say: Stop, please, stop, let me think all of this over. How did I come to be here? Is there not a method by which I may turn time back, and be home?

But they are upon him.

Oh, John!, his friend calls out from nearby and, dying, the boy from Kansas hears this dimly, the last sound he ever hears. (Back in Kansas, the boy's mother, at this exact moment, pauses at the water well, bucket in hand, feeling, briefly, his presence — as she will later say, she will say and say until the last day of her life — with an overlay of such dread and panic that, dropping the bucket, she falls to her knees.)

The cry goes out among the tribes: We can kill them all. Arrows arc up and kill horses and horse-holders. Troopers are pierced through their skulls, necks, eyes. The braves wave blankets to stampede the horses. A warrior's jaw is shot away and he wanders the field disoriented, the lower half of his face missing. This is Three Horn, the man who, at night, warms his wife, Red Deer Woman. She, like the Kansan mother, feels a presentiment of disaster, as she continues to guide their son to safety. Seeing Three Horn thus disfigured, Wooden Leg retreats to a ravine nearby to vomit. The fleeing horses of the Seventh intermix with the ponies of the braves, who have dismounted, the better to seek cover in the countless gullies and washes leading up to the high place to which the final group of whites has fled to make its stand. The dust is thick; it feels like night, though it is only four o'clock in the afternoon.

I clench and unclench my fists nervously, as in: Here we go.

It is nearly time for my Solo.

I stand, nervously priming my pump.

I am to be Lieutenant Henry Harrington, known among the warriors as "the Bravest

Man" for the way he fought in those last frenzied moments, as his command, C Company, tried in vain to rejoin Custer's main force, and who, once it became clear that all under his command were either dead or about to be killed, turned his horse (a magnificent large-chested sorrel) directly into the Indian ranks and rode through the startled braves, away from the battlefield, thundering into an open field to the west.

Two braves broke away from the fight to chase him down (I will Speak, I will Shout). But his mount was superior, and soon he had left the pursuing braves behind. Then, even as they abandoned the chase and slowed their horses to a walk, Harrington inexplicably brought his revolver to his head and —

"Hello, hello!" adult son Mike calls from the doorway of Listening Room. "May I have your attention please?"

Mr. U. hits Pause.

It is a jolt, this abrupt leaving behind of the heat/fear/prairie feel into which we Speakers and Singers have just begun to pleasantly resettle.

"Son," Mr. U. says, his uncertain smile seeming to indicate that he will, of course, be happy to include adult son Mike in this, his moment of triumph, in whatever way

66

adult son Mike would like to be included, although he is also wondering, somewhat, perhaps, why adult son Mike couldn't have said whatever it is he seems to want to say a bit earlier (during Intermission, for example).

Adult son Mike steps to one side of the door and makes a sweeping arm gesture, as in: Look, look who I am welcoming in here.

They come in fast: young men and women in white stocking caps under the raised hoodies of emerald-green sweatshirts, with guns, looking, somewhat, like one of the teen musical ensembles adult son Mike will, when bored, make us watch on his phone.

Their leader urges Company to stay calm. Company does not: two men demand to know what this is, what is this all about, do they not know this is a private home? The leader urges the two men to step into the aisle, speak their minds, he is (they are) here to listen.

"I would hope so," says the more rotund of the two, though both are rotund, then joins the leader in the aisle and extends a hand to his less-rotund friend, who is having some trouble getting out.

Both rotund men are now in the aisle, ready to register their feelings.

The leader raises the gun, shoots them

67

dead, first one, then the other.

What a sound! We Speakers, we Singers, and Company, and Mr. U. and Mrs. U., and adult son Mike all flinch as one, a nest of mice beneath the black shadow of the massive wing of some overflying eagle.

The rotund men are two bleeding heaps on the floor, with seated, screaming wives.

"We are going to bring some decency into this world!" the leader shouts. "Once and for all. It begins tonight."

How can they speak of decency, asks an old woman with young hair, when they have just killed Keith Durtz and Larry Reynolds, both of whom have given abundantly to so many charitable causes? Isn't that right, Leah?

"And he didn't even want to come to this," sobs Leah, wife of the fallen Keith.

The leader grabs the old woman by her young hair, drags her into the aisle.

Would she like to elaborate? On her statement? In which she alleged hypocrisy among this group now holding her life in its hands?

She would not.

He casts her away. She falls to the floor with an inadvertent, melodramatic grace and lies there, eyes open.

Blink, blink, blink.

One among the intruders, a girl in yellow

tennis shoes, begins moving among Company, collecting cellphones in a tie-dyed cloth bag.

Company, the leader announces, will proceed into the basement. In a few hours, help will come and they will be released. They, the White Cap Consortium, understand the concept of differential guilt. Are they, Company, for merely attending an event, as culpable as Mr. and Mrs. Untermeyer? No. Some may, it is true, have Singers and/or Speakers of their own at home. But the Consortium has decided to err in the direction of mercy. Company may rest assured: none of them will be harmed. Not tonight, anyway. But he hopes that those among Company who do, in fact, have Singers and/or Speakers at home will, while down in the basement, reflect upon the role of chance at work tonight; this action is taking place here, in this home (and not in their homes), simply because the Consortium's leadership recently found itself presented with an opportunity, by a certain enlightened party/former classmate (here he gives a playful salute to adult son Mike), but Company may be sure that there will come a time, and let us pray it will be soon, when no family participating in this barbaric, degrading practice will ever feel entirely safe in their home again.

These individuals (he says, indicating we Speakers, we Singers) are not animals, not toys, not playthings. How would Company like it? If they, or their spouse, or one of their children, or one of their parents had his or her memory eradicated via the Morley Procedure (or Morley II, for Singers) and thereby lost all awareness of who they were, how they had lived, what they had valued, whom they had loved, and woke to find themselves mounted on some stranger's Speaking Wall, compelled to perform like a trained beast for the cheap amusement of a braying crowd?

"I'd like to respond," says Mr. U. "But I don't want to be shot. Is that possible?"

"Make it quick," says the girl in yellow sneakers.

"I object to your characterization," Mr. U. says. "No one was coerced. On the contrary, these Speakers, these Singers, they applied. And considered it a great privilege to have been accepted. And are well compensated. Money is sent — believe me, I write the checks every month — to their designees. These folks, honestly? Are like family to us. You people may not like it, but everyone here has consented to this arrangement and, if I may say so, as terrible as you may feel me to be, I have, at least, never killed any-one."

I feel like applauding. Why are these rude individuals here, in our home, with their violence? I do not know about "compensation," or "designees," or any of that but feel proud of Mr. U.'s courage, and confident that his eloquence will save the day.

The intruders appear unmoved.

"Enough," the leader says. "Enough predictable reactionary blather."

"It's not exactly 'volunteering' if you're driven to it by hardship," says the girl in yellow sneakers.

Taking out a notebook, she steps over to Craig.

"Hector," she says. "Wife: Danielle. No kids. Unemployed for seven years. Three poodles: Rudy, Phipps, Esmerelda II."

Then steps over to Lauren.

"Cindy," she says. "A nurse with an unfortunate addiction issue. Also, a kid. A baby. Stuart."

Lauren looks, at first, blank. Then emits a startled nose-snort, as if her bell has been rung.

Company is to proceed to the back of the room, the leader says. No heroics, please, no drama.

To comply, those in the first few rows

71

must step over the two portly corpses. An old man stops to help the old woman (not nearly as old as him) to her feet. Her young hair, a wig, is left behind, where she fell.

Before heading to the basement, the girl in yellow sneakers says, there is something they are going to be asked to witness. For their edification. To encourage them to change their ways. And aid them in seeing the light.

Adult son Mike does not look well. He looks like someone who was perhaps not fully informed, when helping facilitate this, that, for example, two portly men would be shot dead and an elderly woman shoved to the ground so roughly that her young hair would fly off.

"Mike," the leader says. "Where's Mom?"

"She hates these things," Mr. U. says. "She's out of town."

"That's a lie," the leader says. "He told us you'd both be here. Like half an hour ago. When he called to give us the go-ahead. Where's Mom, Mike?"

Adult son Mike's eyes are closed tight and he is slightly swaying.

"He's scared," Mr. U. says. "He doesn't seem to understand what's happening."

"He arranged it, dumbass," the leader says.

72

"I know that," Mr. U. says softly. "Of course I know that."

"I'm for the freedom," adult son Mike says. "But not for the killing."

"Well, you can't be for the freedom and against the killing," says the yellow-sneakered girl.

"Which of you is Angela Untermeyer?" asks the leader.

A long silence falls on Listening Room.

"I am Spartacus," jokes a male member of Company, then, seeming to immediately regret it, covers his mouth with both hands.

"That's her," Lauren says. "Back there."

Mrs. U. sneers, pushes off the wall, joins Mr. U. at the front, takes his hand, brings it to her lips for a kiss.

The leader raises his gun to the head of Mr. U. as the yellow-sneakered girl begins filming on her phone.

"For the crime of the degradation of men and women who, no less than you, deserve lives full of dignity, respect, and autonomy," the leader says, "we sentence you to death."

"What?" shrieks adult son Mike.

"You two to death," says the yellow-sneakered girl.

"We sentence the two of you to death," the leader says, "in hopes that, across the land, others of your ilk, seeing this, will come to understand that the systematic abuse of innocent human beings has consequences."

"Severe consequences," says the yellow-sneakered girl.

"We've never abused anyone in our lives," Mrs. U. says, in a rasp she can barely get out.

"Excuse me, not true," says Lauren.

Everyone looks at Lauren.

"She sexually abuses Jeremy here," she says. "Often."

Everyone looks at me.

"She comes in here at night, makes him Speak to her, while she, you know," Lauren says.

"Self-pleasures," says Craig.

Everyone looks at Mrs. U.

Who is blushing.

"I never," she stammers. "It was . . ."

"It was what?" the yellow-sneakered girl demands.

"Consensual," says Mrs. U.

"How can it be consensual when your victim's been brain-wiped and Pinioned to a Wall and has no memories whatsoever of ever having been out of this room?" the leader says. "Enlighten us."

"It is," I say.

Everyone looks back at me.

"Very much so," I say. "I like it. I like her. I live for it. I love her."

"Oh boy," says the leader. "Someone shut this poor sap down."

What a dummy. I am not even On. We are Paused. This is just me, myself, speaking from the heart.

The yellow-sneakered girl strides to Podium and, messing with something there, takes us, in her ignorance, off Pause, pegging our Intensity not just to high but, it feels like, very highest, where we never go.

I feel the most powerful pre-Pulse I have ever felt.

And am Harrington.

Very much so.

Samuels is writhing in the dirt, arrow in his throat. Riverton, unhorsed by a group of three braves, is the object of three hatchets moving in the sun like pistons. I realize I must break away or die. Here is an opening. I turn my magnificent, large-chested sorrel into the Indian ranks and ride through the startled braves, away from the battlefield, thundering into an open field to the west.

And am free.

Am I being pursued?

I am.

The Singers join in. They have no choice. They too are being Pulsed at very highest

Intensity. Each Sings a different, jagged melody line. As Rehearsed. The intent of their Song: to indicate the agitated state of my mind as I ride. If caught, will I not, as we have often discussed among ourselves, be taken alive and tortured, like Dennison, that poor bastard, found on the trail with his balls pinned to his forehead? I, Harrington, am a fair-minded man, and recognize that this would merely be a case of "turnabout is fair play." I recall seeing, at an exposition in Denver, the genitalia of a Cheyenne woman, obtained by a trooper after the Washita fight, displayed in a glass case. And yet I myself have never participated in such depredations, and "fair play" does not seem like "fair play" when you are the one who, within minutes, is to be made victim of whatever foul, sharp-bladed mischief these fellows intend.

On my magnificent sorrel I begin to leave the braves behind.

But then, even as they abandon the chase and slow their horses to a walk, I inexplicably bring my revolver to my head. Any second now (I Speak) I will fire, killing myself instantly, and my body will lurch off to one side of the sorrel, astonishing the watching braves.

Why will I do it? I ask.

No one can know, I reply.

"Dude, shut it!" someone shouts from far away.

"Ignore him, Darren, Jesus," says a second person.

"I can't hear myself think," the first says frantically.

Perhaps (I Speak, I Shout) my body could not help but flee (the dust, that screaming, the percussive stone-on-meat sound coming from every direction) but now, in flight, it occurs to me that this is cowardice itself: one's body dictating an action with no honorable end. How might this flight be justified, even if I succeed in escaping? When Custer and the others are still, at that moment, as I flee, alive? Mustn't I turn, rejoin the fight? But I can't, I won't, it is too terrible, my legs and arms agree with my horse that *back* is not a direction in which we may go, but my mind, my hero's mind, honor-bound, in love with virtue, knows that I will not be able to live with this, will not be able to ride the hundreds of miles to some outpost of civilization and there lie about what happened (*I was knocked unconscious and woke hours later to find my fellows dead around me*) or honestly confess (*I fled when there was still more I might have done to aid Custer and his men,*

*who were still alive and fighting as I aban-
doned the field*).

It is a terrible conundrum.

There is but one way out, it seems to me,
as I ride: to die at my own hand, thus retain-
ing my honor.

Then one of the pursuing braves pulls up
beside me. Having stepped over from where
he formerly stood. There beside the quak-
ing Untermeyers. He rides beside me now,
gun hanging loosely in his hand at his side.

I reach down, snatch the gun away.

It is so easy.

"Hey, hey," he says, and tries to take it
back. But I am an officer, the Bravest Man,
and the adrenaline of flight is still in me.

And I now have his gun in my hand.

Why not use it?

To save my dear friends the Untermeyers,
surrounded back on Last Stand Hill, at the
point of death, over near Podium?

I move the gun to the head of the brave.
The sun overhead is a dust-dimmed orb.
Up there with the two familiar fire sprin-
klers. The prairie grass sways. Among the
folding chairs. From the hill upon which
my dear friends are about to die, I sense
them urging me to fire, and save them.

I fire.

The brave falls. The second brave dismounts, rushes to the side of the first. He too must die, if I am to save my friends. I shoot, he falls. His feet are crossed, there in his yellow sneakers. Her feet. Her feet, in her yellow sneakers, are crossed. As she dies.

The Singers' Song changes, from Singing to screaming.

The first brave, still moving, gestures for me to come down near his mouth.

I do so.

For, though an enemy, he is, like me, a warrior, a man of action.

"Who were you?" he says, in perfect, unaccented English. "Before this? You were *somebody.* Did you have a wife? Kids? Check the notebook. These people? Not your friends. They have used you and will continue to use and degrade you and thousands of others like you until somebody stops them."

Wife? Kids?

I engage my mind with the fiercest, most honest focus.

And find nothing.

"No," I say. "No wife, no kids. And I think I would remember that."

"You wouldn't," he says. "You absolutely would not. And that's the worst thing these bastards have done to you."

Then dies.

A wife? That is funny. If I had a wife, would I not at least be able to recall her name? Recall the way she moved? Moved around our — our neat yellow house? In the willows, at the end of a dusty lane? Out the side window of which one could glimpse two leaning green chicken coops that always seemed to be conferring with one another, there in the willow-dappled —

Good God, I recall with a jolt of astonishment: I do have a wife. I do! Back in Michigan. Grace Berard. And children: Grace Aileen Harrington, daughter. Harry Berard Harrington, son. Of Clinton. Clinton, Michigan. Sweet Lord, what have I done? Why have I come here? To this village?

I came here to ride over tents full of children, rope together the hands of weeping women.

Children like my children, women like my wife.

And would have done so.

But for the intervention of these two.

These two I have killed.

The Mod now urges me back: the news of Harrington's death (I Speak, I Shout, compelled by the Mod to do so) found Mrs. Harrington at their home in Michigan. She took the news calmly at first but later that evening went missing, leaving the children behind in the empty house. She was not heard from again for two years, during which time she roamed the West, seeking her husband. At one point, she was found wandering the battlefield by members of the Crow tribe: an insane white woman in a torn, filthy dress, the same dress she had been wearing the night she heard of her husband's death, a lost woman, likely made use of by men along the road, degraded by hunger and thirst.

My dear wife.

It is I who did this to you, I who bequeathed you this nightmarish fate.

Why am I even here? I Speak. On this murderous march? Upon this Speaking Wall? Have my thoughts and deeds ever truly been my own? Do I not hang perpetually inert here, until Pulsed? Why must I, and Lauren, and Craig, and our Singers hang here, when even Jean, lowly Jean, even reprehensible adult son Mike, may leave Listening Room whenever they please? Has anyone ever, for my enjoyment, Spoken words I have given them to Speak? Has anyone Sung, even once, for my pleasure?

Then, suddenly, the prairie is gone, and the fear, and I am no longer winded with flight; nor can I smell horses, blood, or sun-scorched, waist-high grass.

I am no longer Harrington. Well, just a bit. Then not at all.

Mr. U. stands at Podium, having switched us Off.

Returning to myself, I feel ashamed. For what I have just now Spoken. I have just now Spoken aloud, publicly, against my craft, my life, against the dear Untermeyers, my family.

If, for merely speaking without permission, one is sent to Penalty shed, what punishment must await me now?

The two I have killed are dead, yet young. One of her yellow shoes is untied. He has, this morning, perhaps nervous about what was to come, missed a belt loop. Might these two, in another life, have been friends of mine? Might they have enjoyed hearing me Speak upon topics of interest to them? Now that can never be. Nothing, henceforth, can be, for them.

And it is I who have done it.

Company shouts their approval: I have saved the Untermeyers from these fanatics who came to murder them.

The remaining members of the White Cap Consortium stand wide-eyed amid the disordered folding chairs. It appears that, all along, only their leader had a gun. That is, the intruders had just that one gun between them.

And I am now holding it.

Company, inspired by my actions, turns upon the intruders, and Listening Room fills with the sounds of punching and oofing, heads being knocked against walls, men choking other men, women gasping, shocked to find themselves yanking back the hair of other women.

Company possesses superior numbers; is imbued with the confidence of wealth; is not inclined to lose, having decided long ago to cushion itself within abundance and thus keep loss at bay.

But then Lauren, dear Lauren, formerly so gentle, strides across Listening Room, punches Mrs. U. in the face, screaming that once she, Lauren, had a baby, baby Stuart. She remembers it all now, bitch! Mr. U. goes to Mrs. U.'s aid and Craig, from behind, kicks him down. The Singers surge forward, wailing melodically. Adult son Mike is left, by them, in a heap by the door; Jed, bleeding from the mouth, struggles to rise from a wall against which two Consortium members have thrown him; Jean, elbowed in the face by the female Singer who earlier required the Ativan but now seems abundantly confident, wanders between two folding chairs, muttering, seemingly lost.

How strange it is to see these dear, familiar friends of mine (Mr. U., Mrs. U., Jean, Jed) brought so low.

By other dear, familiar friends of mine (Lauren and Craig).

The gun hangs heavy in my hand.

I was born not of a gigantic woman but a human-sized mother. I know that now. I, possibly, had a wife. I must have loved her but have no memory of her. Who I love now is Mrs. U., of the lovely biting kiss. I will not see her hurt, for all that we have shared. And do not wish to see Mr. U. hurt, he who has taken me, on so many occasions, to places of such delicious, exalted expressiveness. But also, I do not wish to see Lauren and Craig, lifelong pals and co-creators, hurt, yet know that, should they fail in this, they must bear the full brunt of Company's crushing, retributive power.

Mrs. U. pulls away from Lauren, crawls toward me, somehow elegant even in this.

"Jeremy," she says pitiably. "Please save us."

How can I refuse her, the source of the greatest joy I have ever known? The intruders will kill her. They will. They were on the brink of doing so, and will, should they prevail.

In her (blue-green) eyes, I see: desire, acceptance, a warm assurance that if I hand her the gun, she will do what is right.

For the two of us.

For all of us.

I hand her the gun. She hands it to Mr. U., who orders the White Cap Consortium, Lauren, Craig, and the Singers to the floor. Soon everyone but Company is down there with the fallen portly men and the two I killed, who are posed, now, in death, in attitudes of wild dancing: the yellow-sneakered girl seems to be tossing the notebook across to the leader, who seems about to catch it.

Mr. U. swoops over, plucks up the notebook, tucks it into the pocket of his Performance blazer.

And a great tragedy is thereby averted.

But I must admit I feel rather low after.

The police take Craig, Lauren, the Singers, and the intruders away. Company, having been questioned, drifts out of Listening Room, speaking spiritedly of their satisfaction that justice has prevailed, of the rank hubris of the intruders, of my courage, my admirable presence of mind.

85

"Yeah, you did good, pard," Jed says as, still shaky, he re-Pinions me at floor height, takes out my RoamStar, resettles my head back into my Fahey Cup. "Those dirtbags were animals."

"As for those two," Jean says, glancing over at the two empty Fahey Cups, into which the heads of Craig and Lauren formerly nestled, "they'll be fine. They'll honestly never know what hit them."

Jed and Jean go out. I am left alone.

Gosh, I think, bursting into tears, I never wished to kill anyone and, on the contrary, wished to never even hurt anyone. And now look: I have killed two people. Also on my mind: Craig and Lauren, whose crestfallen looks of betrayal, directed at me as, struggling, they were roughly dragged away, I will not soon forget.

Night falls.

A silent man and woman come with a mop and a cart, to clean up the blood and take away the two I killed.

Thank goodness.

I did it for love, I whisper to myself again and again, as the rising moon makes a light-square around the edges of the boarded-up window, while, on the floor, an associated light-parallelogram moves slowly toward Podium and then, fractured, climbs up it.

Around midnight Mr. U. comes in.

"Can't sleep either, eh?" he says.

I raise my hand.

"Go," he says.

"What will happen to Craig and Lauren?" I say.

"They're getting some help," he says. "At a hospital. Of sorts. Having some work done, to help them forget this whole stupid thing. Well, forget everything, actually. Get them back to square one. So they can begin Speaking again. Here, or elsewhere. I haven't decided."

"Oh," I say.

I hear Mrs. U. out there, moving around Main Living Area.

Mr. U. watches me listening.

"As far as that?" he says. "She won't be coming in here anymore. We've discussed it, she's agreed. That's over. Never again. But if she does? Come in? Call out. That's an order, or whatever. A directive. We're going to try to get our marriage back together. Would you be willing to help me out with that, pal? By, you know, calling out? If she does, uh, weaken and come in here?"

I nod.

"Just so you know?" he says. "I don't blame you. At all. She's a beautiful woman. I get that. How was someone with your, uh, limitations supposed to know anything about restraint, morality, loyalty, and all that? The funny thing is, I don't really blame her either. We'd hit a rough patch. I'd sort of withdrawn. Into my hobby. And you're a nice-looking young guy. I bet you chatted her up good. With your Speaking. Am I right?"

I blush.

"Story of my life," he says. "Hoisted by my own petard."

He takes a pear from his pocket, puts it in my hand.

"No hard feelings," he says. "You woke me up. You did. Woke us up. Saved us. Literally, yes, by, you know, killing those two. That was a big deal, for sure. Where would we be right now without you?"

"Dead," I say.

"Dead, yes, true," he says. "But also, emotionally, where would we be?"

Without me, I think, you would be no-where emotionally, being dead.

"And in case you're wondering, because I know the two of you were close?" he says. "Mikey is with some compassionate relatives. Also getting some help. This has been heartbreaking for him. Obviously."

Then he goes out, halfheartedly straightening a few chairs en route, then giving up, as it is a big and lowly job, best left to the likes of Jean and Jed.

Though tired, I wait up.

For Mrs. U.

Likely he is out there, watching her like a hawk.

Come to me, my love, I think. I have killed in your name. And need to know it was worth it.

Then in she comes.

Yes, here she is, against his wishes.

Standing silently against Podium, she raises one finger to her lips, indicating: Stay quiet.

Ignoring his directive, I do not call out. I want her to know that I am here for her, that I will do with her whatever she desires, even to the ultimate, whatever that is.

"I want to thank you," she whispers, leaning in, smelling good, like a rose if a rose were a bit angry. "You helped me feel good about myself during what was a really bleak time for me. You were a supportive presence at a point in my journey when I literally had no one else in my corner. In a different world, who knows? But in this world? Well, no, of course not. I'm sure, being as intelligent as you are, you fully understood that all along. My hope is that you, in here, will always think of me, out there, as a friend. Though we won't be, uh, interacting much anymore. Or, you know, ever again. Sadly."

Then kisses me on the forehead and goes out.

I wish to follow up with questions. But she, moving rapidly away with her back to me, fails to see my raised hand.

Soon, from Bedroom, I hear sounds, certain harrowing sounds, energetic, ecstatic, conciliatory sounds of the type that might follow closely upon a frightening, clarifying brush with death.

It just goes on and on.

Good thing adult son Mike is not home, I think.

Later, the Bedroom sounds become more hushed and confidential, less like impact and release: whispered promises, soft confessions of admiration, urgent murmurings that signal the flaring back to life of an old and valued bond.

Next morning Jed comes in.

With Craig and Lauren.

"Ed, Sharon," Jed says. "This is Jeremy."

Ed and Sharon nod at me, as in, Hello,

90

new colleague.

They do not seem to remember Listening Room, or me. They just smile shyly as Jed gets their heads nestled into their Fahey Cups.

Mr. U. comes in, smiling, aglow.

"What a morning," he says. "God's in His heaven. And all that happy crap. Man, I feel amazing. What do you say we finish that Custer one off? Getting interrupted like that leaves a bad taste in one's mouth, doesn't it?"

He is talking to me, I guess. Since Ed and Sharon, freshly Pinioned, are hanging there beaming like memory-free idiots, no offense.

But yes: the abrupt truncation of our Performance has left several bowling pins in my air, so to speak. Having been on Last Stand Hill, on very highest Intensity, encircled by enemies, part of me remains there still, with Custer, dreading my death, even as another part remains with Crazy Horse et al., encircling the hill, arcing arrows up into it.

Mr. U. goes to Podium.

I begin.

Again: the thirst, the fear, the smell of blood, horses, summer grass, sun-heated leather. Custer and his men reach the small rise on which they will die. Custer understands that Reno's attack has failed, that he is badly outnumbered, that his famous luck has run out. Visibility is nil, for the dust. In those last moments he becomes keenly aware of his youngest brother, Boston, and his nephew Autie, just eighteen. Boston and Autie are not soldiers but he has allowed them to be here, on a lark, for the sheer adventure of it. Now, for this indulgence, they will die. It is possible he watches them die; it is possible he dies before them and they watch him die. It is possible that, in the dust and the mayhem, none of them sees the other(s) die. No one knows for sure. No one will ever know. But now they are all dying, in the dust, amid the sound of shouting, cursing, wailing, delirious laughter.

Then all falls quiet.

The dust-curtain slowly descends as the warriors move up to see what they have wrought. Some, sickened, go off to sit alone. Others, delirious with victory, give thanks. A few of the older men intuit the truth: this stunning victory is mere prelude; the colossus that is the white nation, galvanized by this humiliation, will soon enact a merciless revenge.

Now Ed and Sharon join me.

The three of us become the women who move among the fallen whites, stripping and mutilating their bodies in order to hamper and annoy their souls in the afterlife. We catalog arrows in rectums, sawed-off genitals sewn into mouths; the complete erasure, with rocks, of the face of Custer's brother Tom; the piercing of one of Custer's eardrums with an awl, for his failure, in life, to listen. This gives us no joy; we know that these, even these, were sons, husbands, fathers, brothers. But our hearts are bad. We hate them, we do, for the aggressive, murderous fools they were. Many of our own sons and husbands and fathers and brothers lie freshly dead at their hands. Why did they come? Why not stay home, loving what was theirs to love, wanting no more than what they had, enjoying the astonishing blessings already laid out before them? It now falls upon us to interrupt the energy of their terrible stupidity; it must not be allowed to flow unrebuked into the next world.

Here our Singers were to have made a sound imitative of the plains wind sweeping over the fallen, the still-mutilating women, the grieving loved ones back in the village, the exhausted, wounded ponies, limping down to the river to drink.

And that was to have been the end.

But because we have no Singers, Listening Room falls silent. Except, Mr. U. begins to weep. To weep in gratitude. She who strayed has now returned. Where there was lovelessness, there is again abundant love. Life will now become, again, what it always was for him, before the recent challenges: a grand adventure, marked by frequent, almost predictable victories; dominion on every front; daily confirmation of his location at the center of the universe.

I look at Ed and Sharon. Their faces reflect the great transport that comes with Speaking for the first time.

How I envy them.

For, whatever Mr. U. may in the future give me to Speak, I will never enjoy it again, any more than would a puppet, picked up off the floor, enjoy the suddenly manipulating hand.

The Mom of Bold Action

Again she found herself spending her precious morning writing time pacing her lovable sty of a kitchen making no progress *at all*. Why was she holding a can opener?

Hmm.

That could be something.

"The Trusty Little Opener." Gerard the Can Opener was a dreamer. He wanted to open BIG things. BIGGER things. The BIGGEST things! But all he ever got to open was, uh, beans? Corn? Tuna?

You had to give him something essential to open, to save the day. Medicine? Heart medicine? You did not open heart medicine with a can opener. Tomato paste? Some beloved person in the household really longed for spaghetti? Old Italian gal. Friend to all. On her last legs. The spaghetti brought her back to Florence or whatever? But the modern, high-tech can opener, Cliff, was out partying with a wicked colander and a cynical head of lettuce. Gerard saw his chance. Even though he dated back to the 1960s and didn't have a fancy rubber handle like Cliff, he could still open stuff. This was it! His chance to help dear sweet Mama Tinti get her final, pre-death bowl of —

Ugh.

Honestly.

Why was Mr. Potts going nuts behind the gate in the mudroom? She'd already given him three of those peanut-butter thingies.

"The Discontented Dog." The Discontented Dog was never happy. No matter how many peanut-butter thingies he was given. When he was in, he wanted out. When out —

She grabbed another peanut-butter thingie from the box.

"The Peanut-Butter Thingie Who Sacrificed Himself So the Other Peanut-Butter Thingies in the Box Could Live." Jim the Peanut-Butter Thingie pushed his peanut-shaped body higher and higher, toward the questing human hand. Jake and Polly watched, amazed. Was Jim *trying* to get eaten? "Go on, live your dreams, you two!" Jim shouted as a thumb and a finger grasped him around his, uh, slender place. The place that, for Peanut-Butter Thingies, served as a waist.

She moved the gate, gave Mr. Potts the peanut-butter thingie, leaned out the door, called for Derek to come put Mr. Potts on the tie-out.

No reply.

"The Son Who Failed to Reply." Once upon a time, there was a son who, when called, failed to reply. Was he deliberately ignoring her? Because pre-adolescent? Was he masturbating yet? Was that her business? The mother faithfully checked underwear/ sheets for signs of masturbation, so that, as needed, she could let him know, in her quiet way, that everyone, even famous people, even our great, historical —

"A Time for Oneself." George Washington, twelve years of age, lay in his bed. A four-poster, which had been made, as all beds were back then, by hand. Was it weird? What he'd been imagining? Their neighbor Mrs. Betsy Alcott, in that form-fitting bodice, reaching over to take off his tricorn hat? No: if a person felt something, it was, by definition, "normal." If he found himself touching himself while imagining the slender Mrs. Alcott bringing her quill pen absentmindedly to her full lips, no doubt other little boys in other times and places had felt inclined to touch themselves while imagining similar things. Therefore, it was fine, what he was doing! He suddenly felt so free and, feeling free, began to dream of a new land, a land where all could feel as free as —

Lord. Nearly noon.

Time to sit down and actually write something.

Where was Derek, though? Seriously? She worried. As a baby, he'd had a collapsed lung.

You good? she'd called out last night, from bed.

You're turning him into a nervous wreck, Keith had said.

I'm fine, Derek had called from his room. Also, not deaf.

Lungs still going? Keith said.

Far as I can tell, Derek said.

We just worry, she said. We love you so much.

Right back atcha, Derek said.

Then there'd been this sweet silence.

She adored it. Having a family. TV families were always fricked up, but hers was something else entirely. They liked one another. Had so much fun. Trusted one another and confided in one another and accepted one another just as they were, no matter what.

98

Not out front, not out back.

What the hell, seriously? He'd promised to stay in the yard. And this was a kid who never broke a promise.

"The Boy Whose Bad Lung Conked Out in the Woods."

"The Boy Who Lay Feebly Calling Out for His Mom."

"The Boy Who Died Utterly Alone and Became One with the Spirits of the Forest."

And evermore the mother wandered the woods, seeking her lost boy.

Eek.

"The Mom Who Rushed into the Woods but Once There Forgot How to Do CPR but Then Suddenly Remembered."

Oh God, oh God. Her cheeks were so hot.

Derek was hurt somewhere. She just knew it. A mother knew these things.

She grabbed her cellphone and the first-aid kit and —

Wait, whoa, hold on.

This right here was what Keith was always talking about. She was freaking out. She had a tendency to get worked up. Sometimes a mother did *not* just know these things. Last month, she'd just known that he'd been abducted from the bus stop. She'd raced down there in her bathrobe and house slippers. He'd seen her coming. Started shaking his head, like, Ma, no, no, no. But too late. The older boys were already imitating her shuffling run.

Once she'd dreamed he'd started smoking. In the dream, he'd been smoking a cigar. At Cub Scouts. Sort of flaunting it. He had a man's voice and, in that voice, asked Mr. Belden if there was such a thing as a Smoking Merit Badge. Next morning, in real life, he'd busted her sniffing his clothes and started bawling the way he did when he was totally telling the truth but not being heard.

"Why would I *smoke*?" he'd said. "Ma, that's dis*gust*ing."

What you had to do was overrule your irrational fears. By learning the facts. She'd read about this in *Best Life.* One gal scared of flying had spent the month before her trip to China memorizing air-fatality statistics. A man afraid of snakes had come up with a mantra about the majority of snakes being non-venomous. In another article, parents, intending the best, had gone too far. One mom, super-focused on eating right, had turned her daughter anorexic. A dad had been too strict about violin practice and now his son hated music. Also, had panic attacks whenever near polished brown wood.

All over the world right now, thousands of boys were out farting around, having broken a promise they'd made to stay in the yard.

Most woods were not dangerous.

Generally, lungs did not just fail.

The world was not a scary or hostile place, and Derek was a smart little guy with a good head on his shoulders.

He was fine. What she was going to do was sit down and write something.

What she was not going to do was hover by the window.

Much.

"The Tree Who Longed to Come Inside." Once there was a tree who longed to come inside and sit by the woodstove. He knew this was weird. He knew that his fellow trees were being cruelly burned in there. But, gosh, the kitchen looked so inviting. Because of all the hard work the mother had done. Painting and whatnot. When she should have been writing. The smoke pouring out of the chimney smelled so nice. The flesh of his fellow trees, burning, smelled amazing.

Yikes.

Restart.

Once there was a tree who longed to come inside. Tim the Tree felt so drawn to people. Even as a sapling, he'd just loved hearing them talk. Gosh, what was a "transmission leak"? What did the daddy mean by "You obsess too much"? What did the mommy mean by saying that "obsessing" was her "super-power," which she "used every day, in her work"? There were so many words to learn! What was "apology," what was "perturbed," what was "darling"? If the wind was blowing from the east, bending him slightly to the left, he could peer into the kitchen through the dirty little window over the sink, which hadn't been washed in ever so long, through which the mommy was now gazing out at him, a worried look on her —

Restart.

Tim the Tree loved his spot near the path into the woods, from which he could watch the comings and goings of the various forest denizens, large and small, such as bears, foxes, hikers, hunters, and, today —

A strange tableau.

That phrase just popped into her head. Derek walked into the yard. Stumbled. Blood on his face. Holy crap. Weaving like a little drunk.

She burst out of the house, followed by Mr. Potts, who, barking insanely, plowed right through the garden. She plowed through the garden herself, picked Derek up, plowed back through the garden, dropped onto the porch steps with him in her arms.

What happened, baby? she said. Baby, what happened?

Old guy, he said.

Old guy? she said. What old guy?

He came up behind me, he said. Pushed me down.

Where? she said.

Derek didn't want to say.

Sweetie, where were you? she said.

Church Street, he said.

That was — oh, my God, that was nearly downtown. Way disallowed.

Now was not the time.

She got him inside. Nose not broken. No teeth chipped. She called Keith at work. Called the police. Cleaned up Derek's face. It looked like he'd been clawed.

He just . . . pushed you down? she said.

Into a bush, he said.

Must have been a rose or blackberry.

Jesus.

Ten minutes later, Keith walked in.

What's all this? he said.

Her phone rang.

The police had a guy. Already. Old guy. Kind of out of it. They'd found him wandering back and forth between Church and Bellefree. Would she come down, have a look? Bring the kid, if he was up for it?

Oh, he's up for it, she said.

Guy was old, all right.

Long hair, missing tooth, gross sandals, eyes roaming anxiously all over the place.

Of course he denied it. Why would he push a kid down? He was just going through a rough patch right now. But that didn't mean he'd push a kid down. This false accusation was *part* of it. Had Glenda started this? Glenda had a network, of which it seemed the police were part. Also Jimmy Carter was part of it.

She and Keith and Derek and the cop watched on the cop's laptop as the guy was questioned.

I can't be sure, Derek said.

The cop gave her and Keith a look, like: He's going to need to be sure.

Oh, come on, what were the odds? An old guy pushes a kid down, and half an hour later an old guy's found a block away, off his rocker?

Well, now was the time for some parenting.

Some subtle guidance.

If this guy walks out of here, sweetie, she said, don't you think it's possible that he'll push some other kid down? And that kid

104

might end up with more than just a few scratches?

Someone who'd do something like that needs help, pal, Keith said. And the only way he's going to get it is for us to start that process here and now.

How will it help him to be in jail? Derek said.

The look on the cop's face said, Well, good point.

Maybe he'll get some counseling in there, she said.

A grown man pushes a kid down for no reason, there's something wrong, Keith said.

Kind of irresponsible to just let that go, she said.

Derek asked for a couple minutes to think it over.

Dear little guy.

A landline rang in a suboffice and the cop went in there to answer it.

"The Tough Decision." The boy sat in a silver desk chair, nervously swiveling, tracing one of the scratches on his face with his little finger. His mother, pretending to read a bulletin board so she wouldn't seem to be pressuring the lad, felt badly that he'd been put in this position by — that fucking bastard. Toothless hippie bastard. She should have bolted into the interrogation room and pushed his old ass down. Seen how he liked it. Although he was big. And you could tell from his face he had a mean streak.

The cop stepped out of the suboffice faster than . . . well, faster than you'd expect a cop to step out of a suboffice. He came out fast, went right past them, backed up. Like in a cartoon. You expected his rubbery tie to come zinging out of the suboffice a few seconds later.

Well, this takes the cake, he said.

What does? she said.

There's another, he said.

Another what? she said.

Old guy, he said. Over on Church. Wandering around. They're bringing him in.

The second old guy was nearly identical to the first. They could have been brothers. Old hippie, long hair, sandals, missing a tooth.

Different tooth.

But still.

She and Keith exchanged a look, like: Huh.

Second guy also claimed innocence. Seemed maybe slightly more lucid than the first. He had this wad of duct tape he was manhandling. Why didn't the cop take it away? Maybe it was considered a "posses-sion"? Maybe he was "within his rights" to be tossing it distractedly from hand to hand?

Jesus.

This country.

They brought the first guy back and the two old hippies sat side by side, seemingly wary of each other. She felt that each, in his mind, was making the case for being the more intelligent and authentic washed-up former hippie.

Derek was about to cry. She could tell. It was too much pressure.

I honestly don't know, he whispered.

So she shut it down. And that was that. The two old freaks were free to go. She watched them from the window. They hit the lawn and darted off in different direc-tions, fast, like minnows when you put your hand in the water.

At least we didn't put the wrong person in jail, Derek said in the car on the way home.

Long silence.

Well, yes and no, she felt. One of them had done it. Pushed Derek down. Had actu-ally done it. Stepped up, pushed him down. Then sandal-flapped away, all pleased with himself. That had, for sure, happened in this world. Put both in the slammer, you'd be fifty percent right. Now? One hundred percent wrong. And who was suffering? Her little guy. Who was not suffering? Whichever one of them had done it. He was out there right now, bopping around town, crazy thoughts ramped up by this little victory, proof (to him) that his worldview was, like, visionary or some such shit.

Unbelievable.

Damn it.

"The Mom of Bold Action." It was surprisingly easy to get the gun. She wore the yellow dress, hair in a ponytail. She looked pretty but regular. The guy at the store applauded her intention to take lessons. He handed the [insert name of type of gun] right over. Could he please show her how to load it? He could. He did. Now she was driving slowly up Church. Here was the guy. The old hippie. Whichever one had done it. Seeing the gun, he confessed. No. She drove up behind him. There he was, about to shove down another kid. A little girl. In her Communion dress. It was just his thing, pushing kids down. Who knew why? Maybe he'd been pushed down himself as a —

No, nope.

He was just a sicko.

She hopped out of the car, dropped to one knee, took aim. *Blam.* Direct hit. In the leg.

Which, being compassionate, she'd intended. Amazing how good a shot she was. Never having shot before. Well, she'd always been athletic. Down he went. Wounded, he confessed. Begged for mercy. But didn't really seem all that sorry. Was he messing with her? Was there a trace of mockery in his eyes as he fake-apologized? She pressed the gun against his sweaty forehead.

Jeez, Jesus, what was she —

They were driving along the river. A kayaker was paddling against the current, shouting, either nuts or on his phone. Derek was in the back, slumped against the door, looking pensive and deflated, feeling bad, she could tell, for not being sure which guy it had been, for causing this weird silent tension in the car.

Which, she suddenly realized, was still going on.

I think you did perfect, she said. That was not easy, and you handled it beautifully.

Amen, Keith said.

I just wish I could remember, he said. I keep going over it in my mind.

And? Keith said.

Well, he was definitely wearing jeans, Derek said.

The car pulled up to their same old house.

Which now seemed sad. The House of the Victims. The past year, they'd re-roofed it, put on a new porch. For what? What was the big thing they were striving to be part of? Was it good? Did it make any sense? They'd done all that for what? So their kid could get pushed down by some freak? This was, so far, the biggest thing that had ever happened to them as a family.

The other houses in the neighborhood blinked the eyes that were their windows.

Better you than us, they thought.

"The House That Found Itself Suddenly Ostracized."

"The House Made Lonely Through No Fault of Its —"

Crap. Blah. Stupid.

The three of them sat there a bit in the ticking car.

I know I wasn't supposed to be downtown, Derek said. I just wanted to try it.

Fair enough, Keith said.

Such a good dad. Reasonable man. Dear heart. Always fine with — well, everything. Even this, apparently. Fine with Derek breaking his promise. Fine with some random creep assaulting their kid and walking away scot-free.

She felt — if she was being totally honest? — that, back at the station, Keith had, well,

110

not failed them, exactly. She wouldn't go that far. But hadn't there been a time, back in the old days, when Keith, the powerful man of the house, would've pulled aside the other powerful man, the cop, and, between them, a deal would have been struck, and the two freaks would've been quietly led outside for a little "talk" and, oops, while out there, had the living shit beat out of them?

Both of them?

Just to be sure?

Well, that wasn't the best.

That wasn't, you know, fair.

Or whatever.

But jeez. Neither one of those losers was exactly hitting the ball out of the park. For the sake of argument, let's say that Keith and the cop, choosing to err slightly on the side of pro-activity, had (lightly, performatively) roughed up those two dopes. The one who'd done it? Wouldn't do it again. The one who hadn't done it — well, if, in the future, he ever considered doing something out of line, which he probably would, given the life he was leading, he'd think twice. Net result? A safer Church Street. Down which a nice kid like Derek could walk. Derek, in her mind, ambling down this old-timey Church Street, waved to an elderly couple drinking iced tea on their porch. Go around back, lad, use the tire swing on the old apple tree! the husband said. His wife was up there knitting. You remind us of our own son, now a successful doctor! she said, then dropped her yarn ball, which rolled off the porch, and the old guy made a joke about his back as he hobbled down the stairs to fetch it.

Good people.

Salt of the earth.

But Church Street did not belong to them. Or Derek. It belonged to those two freaks, who, because freaky, were somehow the most powerful players in the whole idiotic deal. Why were rejects running the show? Seriously? It was all backward, because nobody wanted to hurt anybody's feelings, nobody was willing to say what they really thought, nobody cared enough to take a stand for what was right.

And things kept spiraling downward.

They walked to the porch through a pile of leaves. Which was no fun. Not today. Today, it was one more thing they had to do to get to the next not-fun thing. Which was dinner.

This was real. This had happened. A guy had attacked her kid and suffered no consequences whatsoever and was probably off bragging about it to some other deadbeats around a campfire or whatnot.

And what was she doing about it?

Going inside to meekly boil pasta.

After dinner, she started writing some of this down. It was easy. It just flowed. It came straight from the heart. An essay. "Justice," she called it. Goodbye, can openers with big dreams; goodbye, talking trees; goodbye, Henry the Dutiful Ice-Cream-Truck Tire, that piece of crap she'd worked on for most of last year; goodbye, forced optimism; goodbye, political correctness. This was the real shit. Wow. She knew just what to say. It was like walking across a creek and rocks kept appearing beneath her feet. It was like speaking out loud. But on paper. It was the most honest, original thing she'd ever written. It didn't sound like her, and yet it *was* her, for real.

Bang, yes, perfect.

She wrote late into the night.

In the morning, she came down to find Keith reading her pages. Her essay. Like, really reading it. She stood in the doorway watching. Well, this was new. This was different. Usually he read her work with this pained look on his face and afterward he'd say she had "a wild imagination" and had

113

"clearly really been into it," although it was
"probably just over his head," because he
was "a dunce with no literary training."

Good? she said today.

Wow, he said.

His face was red and his leg was bouncing
under the table.

Ha. That was nice. That was — flattering.
She was totally wiped out this morning, but
so what? She drifted into the kitchen, tidied
up the little writing desk they'd bought at
Target. So it would be ready. For the next
burst. Keith yelled that he was going for a
run. Wow. Keith hadn't gone running in
years. It was as if reading her essay had
made him want to be as good at something
as she was at writing. Not to brag. But that
was what good writing did, she realized: you
said what you really thought and it made a
kind of energy, and that sincere energy
flowed into the mind of the reader. It was
amazing. She was an *essayist.*

All these years she'd just been working in
the wrong genre.

It had taken this terrible thing happening
to Derek to make that clear. She wouldn't
have chosen it. But it had happened. And
now she had to honor it.

She sat down to write.

Her phone rang.

Story of her life.

They'd caught the second guy, the cop said, the one with the duct-tape ball, breaking into a car, and he'd confessed to pushing Derek down. The cop read her the guy's statement: "Yeah, I pushed him down. He seemed like a smug little shit. I don't know why I did it, really. But he lived. And now maybe he's not so smug. I bet not. You're welcome."

It's actually kind of funny, the cop said. They're cousins.

Who? she said.

The, uh, two suspects, he said. You know Dimini's? The furniture store? Gus Dimini's their uncle.

Wow, Dimini's. They'd bought their TV there. Nice place. Fading place. Their big thing was, on St. Patrick's Day, they gave away green socks. Called themselves "O'Dimini's" for the week. It had been an Irish neighborhood when she was a kid. Now it was — who knew what it was? Everything down there was boarded up. You'd see a huddle of shopping carts on a lawn. A wading pool full of crankshafts. The occasional Confederate flag. But Gus Dimini was a sweetie. Big round man, full white beard. Roaming benevolently around the place like it was a restaurant. Like he

115

was about to seat you at one of his outdoor patio suites.

She should march in, identify herself as a good customer, who, over the years, had spent literally thousands of dollars in there. Demand that he do something. About his low-life nephews. Well, it hadn't literally been thousands. Just that one TV. On clearance. So, like, three hundred dollars. Point was, she was a *customer*. Maybe she should organize a boycott. Among who, though? Whenever she drove past, the delivery van was the only vehicle in the lot. And sometimes Gus would be out there, sitting on a parking bumper, head in hands.

Anyway, it wasn't his job to control his stupid nephews.

She thought of Ricky. Her cousin. Who, on the day he was supposed to get married, had gotten wasted and thrown a tire iron through the window of a sporting-goods store and gone inside to sleep it off. They'd found him next morning, a catcher's mitt on each hand. Ricky had gotten three girls pregnant in the same month and, in a fight with two of their dads at the same time, had broken one dad's nose and had his ribs broken by the other. He'd stolen a car — different time of life, many years later, when he was already the father of two (grown) kids — and driven to, or at least toward, California, but in Ohio had mouthed off to some bikers at a rest stop and been shipped back in a full-body cast, and then had assaulted a nurse in the hospital, after which, while in detention, he'd had a stroke and died.

Had they, had she, tried talking to Ricky? God, yes, over and over, every time she saw him. He'd be moved to tears, promise to change, then ask to borrow some money to start his auto-repair shop. His big idea was, he'd check the whole car over. How that was a big idea, she didn't get. When you declined to loan him the money, he'd say: So you're just like everybody else. A week later, you'd hear that he'd stolen a go-kart and driven it into a lake, or said some racist thing out loud at church, or overdosed, died, come back from the dead, overdosed again, raced out of the hospital, and tried to break into a parking meter.

In time, they'd all given up on him. Except Aunt Janet, who'd had her own struggles (brandy, night panics) but had never given up on Ricky, even after he was dead. She'd funded a little corner of the library, the Ricky Rodgers Memorial Reading Nook, and stocked it with books on substance abuse and Christianity and auto repair.

At least Ricky had never pushed a kid down. Well, that she knew of. Although he had punched an usher after saying that racist thing at church. And had, at one point, toward the end of his life, impregnated a seventeen-year-old. And burned down the grocery store the gal's father owned, after a cashier refused to let him go into the back room and pick through the stuff they were about to throw away. His plan was to take the stuff home for free, charge the store twenty bucks for his trouble.

That was Ricky.

Ah, Ricky, she thought. She'd been crazy about him when they were little. He was just a few years older than her. He'd been so fun. Not bad yet, not really, just energetic, tossing M-80s in the direction of the henhouse, putting spiders in Aunt Janet's slippers.

And now he was dead.

A dead, arrogant, loudmouthed, thoughtless, quasi-pedophilic, racist idiot.

Who, for a while, she'd thought was the greatest.

All these years, in her mind, she'd been defending Ricky, feeling sympathy for Ricky, or trying to, but you know what? Fuck Ricky. She thought about that pregnant seventeen-year-old's dad, that gut-punched usher, the owner of that sporting-goods store. Fuck Ricky. Someone should have dropped a rock on that idiot long ago.

I mean, yes, okay — some rocks had definitely been dropped on Ricky. Jail, foreclosure on that little dump on Webster he'd somehow cobbled together the money to buy, jail again, the bikers, that dad who'd broken his ribs, the group of parishioners at the church who'd knocked out his front teeth in the narthex, because, it turned out, the usher he'd punched had cancer and was the nicest guy in the world and had given a kidney to the pastor a few years earlier and they all loved him.

But it hadn't been enough, none of it had been enough, to get Ricky to pull head out of ass.

An image came into her mind: Ricky, in Hell, in those filthy coveralls he used to wear (which he'd stolen from the one auto shop where he'd managed to hold a job for more than a month), on fire, tears running down his face.

And he was small. So small. She could fit him in the palm of her hand.

Are you sorry? she said. For all that you did? Truly sorry?

Ginnie, it's so hot down here, he said.

But are you sorry? she said.

For what? he said.

Still stupid, still stubborn. Of course, that's why he was in Hell.

He'd been born stupid and stubborn and stayed stubborn and stupid because he was so stupid and stubborn.

Kind of unfair.

She lifted him out of Hell and put him in Heaven. Everything was pure and white up there. Right away he started angrily pacing around, leaving greasy footprints all over the place. The angels looked at her like, You want to get this character out of here?

She closed both hands around Ricky like he was a little mouse, and really focused, and burned all his greasiness away and was able to see, by reading his mind, that he was now, because of her loving focus, a different person. No trace of the old Ricky remained. No trace of the real, original Ricky.

She put him back in Heaven and he stood there, stunned, whoever he was.

She heard Keith galumph up onto the porch.

So much for writing time.

He burst in, flushed and sweaty, bandanna over one shoulder.

Good run? she said.

I didn't go on a run, he said.

120

True, weird, he was wearing khakis.

He'd found the guy, the first guy, he said, the one averse to Jimmy Carter, and had given him one in the knee. With Derek's autographed bat. It hadn't — it hadn't gone that well. The guy had nearly taken the bat away from him. He'd managed to nail him, but just that once. Sort of a, you know — glancing blow? And the thing was, during it? His bandanna had slipped down. And the guy had recognized him. Hey, you're that dad dude, he'd said, in a tone of wonder, holding his knee. So. There was that. The plan was, had been, you know — take down both guys. Like in her essay? Teach them a lesson. About rules. About order. About "reverencing justice." But after that first hit? The sound it made? The wind had sort of gone out of his sails. The bat was in the river. He'd dropped it off the bridge. They'd have to get Derek a new one. And get it signed. By who, though? Did she — did she remember who'd signed it?

Then he collapsed on the couch, burst into tears. His face went all shriveled-apple and he started soundlessly, in slow motion, pounding his fist into the arm of the couch.

Like in her essay?

What the hell?

Wait, she said. Which guy? Did you hit?

121

The first one, he said. The one they brought in first.

She told him about the confession. That the second one had confessed. That he'd essentially, uh, kneecapped the wrong guy.

Oh, great, he said, as if the unfair thing had been done to him.

Derek came down.

Why is Dad crying? he said.

His aunt died, she said.

Which aunt? Derek said.

One you don't know, she said.

How would I not know an aunt of Dad's? he said.

Keith got up, went into the basement. What was he going to do down there? There was nothing down there but the washer and the dryer and a broken treadmill. Was he planning to do laundry? Probably. Sometimes he did that. When upset.

Pretty soon, she heard both washer and dryer going.

God.

Unusual man.

Can I send a note to Dad's uncle? Derek said.

She could tell he knew she was lying.

He's dead, too, she said. He died in a tragic hot-air-balloon accident.

Oh, that uncle, Derek said.

Look, she said. How about go up to your room?

Did Dad hit someone with a bat? Derek said.

Well, she said.

The guy who pushed me down? he said.

She thought about it a second.

Yes, she said.

He seemed pleased, slid across the floor in his socks, mimed a baseball swing.

Over on the Target desk was her essay.

Sitting there all proud of itself.

She sat down, started reading. It was — God. It was so bad. So harsh. It made no sense. Today. She was good — she was a good writer and all that, so, yes, it sort of flowed, but when you really broke it down, saw what it was actually saying —

Wow, Jesus.

She tore the pages in half, dropped them into the garbage, took the bag out of the can, took the bag to the can around the side of the house.

No more essays.

No more writing at all.

She could do more good in the world by, like, baking.

She sat on the porch swing. Imagined the guy Keith had hit, the innocent guy, jogging up the block, dropping down on the porch steps.

Look, she said, it's not that big a deal, right? You seem totally fine. It was, uh, a glancing blow. And wouldn't you have done the same? If it was your kid?

No, he said. I would not have hit a totally unrelated guy with a bat just because he looked like the guy who did it.

Well, yes, she said. Very admirable. But it's easy to say that, when you weren't actually in that —

That's called character, he said.

I didn't do it, she said. Keith did it.

The guy raised his eyebrows. Somehow he knew about that stupid essay.

Words matter, he said.

Oh, shut up, she said.

Now the shit was going to hit the fan. The system was about to come crashing down on them. On the good people. Who'd always, up until now, done everything right. Or at least had tried to.

From inside, her phone rang.

Perfect.

Same cop.

Little issue, he said. Leo Dimini came in here just now. Said he got attacked. With a bat. By someone he claimed was your

124

husband. Would you know anything about that?

Attacked? she said. With a bat?

The falseness in her voice hung there, being mutually considered by the two of them.

I'm going to take that for a no, the cop said.

Keith is a good guy, she said.

He seemed like it, the cop said. But tell him — you know. No more baseball.

No more baseball, she said.

And if I could suggest something? he said.

Okay, she said.

Maybe we let it drop, he said. The, uh, pushing allegation. Might simplify things. The family's been talking among themselves. The idea is, you drop it about the pushing, they drop it about the bat attack. And Babe Ruth over there can, you know, sleep. Easy. Easier. And you, too.

In that instant, she saw it: God, she loved her life so much. The family of ducks that sometimes came waddling across the yard like they owned the place. The way Derek had recently started eating dinner with his winter hat on, elbows on the table, like a little trucker. Last week, Keith had arranged the plastic mini-animals on the windowsill (giraffe, cow, stork, penguin, elk) in a circle around a corn kernel and, in the elk's antlers, had stuck a Post-it note: "Worship-ping some mysterious object."

How do we do that? she said. Drop it?

You just tell me to drop it, he said.

Now? she said.

Now works, he said.

After she hung up, she went down to the basement. Keith was sitting in an old lawn chair. There was a big pile of clean laundry on the deck of the treadmill.

So, asshole just walks, he said.

Unless you buy a new bat and find him and hit him with it, she said.

It was supposed to be funny, but she could see he wasn't ready.

She reached for his hand. He took it, gave it a squeeze.

Give me a minute, he said.

Sure, she said.

In a way, they were lucky. Derek's face would heal. It would. The scratches were light. That guy could have taken the bat away from Keith and nailed him with it. Keith could have swung at the guy's head and killed him. Now, with this one conces-sion, everything could go back to normal.

And it did.

A week passed, another week, a month.

Then, just before Christmas, she found

herself stopped at a light downtown.

Over on the sidewalk, near the war monument, was the guy. One of the guys. She couldn't tell which.

Those two fuckers really were pretty much identical.

Then the other one came out from behind a maintenance shed, yapping away, dragging, on a leash of Christmas lights, a plastic reindeer he'd likely nabbed off somebody's lawn.

That was — wow. That was quite a limp. Quite a limp he had.

Quite a limp he had somehow gotten.

The two of them went off into the woods, having a good old time, arms around each other's shoulders, the two-person unit itself now seeming to have a limp, reindeer bouncing along in pursuit.

Someone behind her blasted his horn. She hit the gas, surged across the bridge.

Her face was suddenly hot. With shame. Oh God, oh shit. She'd done that. They had. Crippled an old fellow. Innocent old fellow. She'd made — well, she'd made an already unfortunate person's crappy life that much harder.

She had.

For real.

God, the hours of her life she'd spent trying to be good. Standing at the sink, deciding if some plastic tofu tub was recyclable. That time she'd hit a squirrel and circled back to see if she could rush it to the vet. No squirrel. But that didn't prove anything. It might have crawled off to die under a bush. She'd parked the car and looked under bush after bush until a lady came out of a hair salon to ask if she was okay.

Walking through the mall, trying to offer a little positive vibe to everyone she passed. Refilling the dog's water because there were floaters in it. As if he cared. But maybe, on some level, he did. Maybe clean water made his life better? Incrementally? Sometimes she'd refold Derek's little shirts two or three times, wondering which way he'd find easiest to unfold. It mattered. Didn't it? When a shirt unfolded nicely and went right on, didn't that maybe give a kid an extra little burst of confidence?

How many shirts did you have to thoughtfully refold and how many staples did you have to pick up off the floor so nobody would get a staple in the foot and how many hours did you have to spend in the store trying to decide which fruit punch had the least high-fructose corn syrup and how many frazzled young moms with babies did you have to let cut in front of you at the post office and how many rude rejection letters did you have to decline to respond to just as rudely and how many nice familial meals did you have to put together while a great story idea sat dying in your mind, to offset one case of hobbling a hapless old —

The world was harsh. Too harsh. Make one mistake, pay for it the rest of your life. She thought of Mary Tillis, who'd rear-ended that minivan and two kids had died. Of Mr. Somers, who'd done something weird with the heater and gassed his elderly parents. Of that guy with the eye patch at Boy Scouts, who'd sloppily secured a load of firewood and then a chunk flew through this lady's windshield and she'd driven off the bridge into the river and drowned while trapped in her car.

What was that guy's sin, the sin that had ruined his life, so that now, at Scouts, he was nearly always drunk and during Pinewood Derby he'd gone charging out the exit door when one of the little cars flipped, leaving his kid, Maury, standing there like, That's just my dad, sorry, he once killed a lady?

One bad knot.

Nine stupid pages.

Fuck.

She hated this feeling. This guilty feeling.

She couldn't live with it.

The parkway was curving west, looping her away from the river into a region of failing strip malls and three lavish megachurches in a row.

That time with the squirrel, she'd gone home, confessed to Keith. They had a habit of mutual confession. Keith always forgave her, then contextualized her sin. Squirrels died all the time, he'd said. We're constantly killing thousands of living things (bugs), every time we drive. But what are we supposed to do? Not drive? Once Keith forgave her, it was only a matter of time before her guilt would start to fade. Even when she'd been crushing so bad on Ed Temley from church, she'd confessed to Keith. Well, Ed's hot, Keith had said, even I can see that, and the day we stop noticing hot people we're pretty much corpses, right?

She imagined sitting across from Keith at the kitchen table.

Oh, hon, by the way? she'd say. Turns out? We gave that innocent old guy a limp. Which he'll take to his grave. So.

Keith would just sit there, stunned.

Maybe we offer to pay his hospital bill, he'd finally say. Or set him up with, you know, an orthopedic surgeon? Something like that?

Well, that opened some doors you didn't want opened. This was not a hippie with insurance. They'd be paying out of pocket. For his surgery. And there would go Derek's college money. That they'd worked so hard to save. And which wasn't going to be enough, anyway. If they kept saving at the current rate, they'd be good for freshman year, maybe. If the school wasn't great. There were limits. To what one could do. She'd fucked up, they'd fucked up, but they weren't gods, they were people, limited, emotional people who sometimes made ill-advised —

That guy was — you know what?

He was not getting their money.

That was one step too far. That was unreasonable. Kind of weird.

Neurotic.

Overinvolved.

She pulled up to the house. It looked crisp. Clean. All the work they'd done really had made it nicer.

A flock of geese came out of a low cloud, emitting this weird, non-goose sound. A second group joined from the left and a third from the right and the greater flock flew off imperfectly in the direction of the high school.

She imagined a beam of white light shooting out of her forehead, an apology beam, charged with the notion *I am so sorry,* that traveled across town and crossed the river and roamed through the woods until it found the two guys and, having briefly paused above them because they looked so damned similar, entered the innocent one. Instantly he knew her. Knew her pain. Knew about Derek's lung thing and how out of step he was with his classmates, how he sometimes went to school with a stuffed bear in his shirt pocket, as if he thought that was a good look, poor dear, and the thing was, knowing her this completely, it all made sense to the guy. And there it was: forgiveness. That's what forgiveness *was.* He was her. Being her, he got it all, saw just how the whole thing had happened.

How could he be mad at her when he *was* her?

A green forgiveness beam shot out of his forehead and flew back over the town, charged with the notion *To tell the truth, I never expected much from life anyway, and, given all the crap that's happened to me, most of which I caused, a slight limp is, believe me, the least of my worries. Plus, the pain is making me really attentive to every moment.*

The beam entered the car, hung there near the glove compartment.

132

Although I do have one request, it said.

Go ahead, she thought kindly.

Forgive my cousin, the beam said. *As I have forgiven you.*

Oh, brother. In a pig's ass.

Like that was happening.

Someday, maybe. Although probably not. She didn't have that in her. Just didn't. She hated that jerk. And always would.

You forgave Ricky, the beam said.

Your guy's no Ricky, she said.

Ricky was worse, the beam said.

Well, she said. If you knew Ricky.

If you knew my cousin, the beam said.

Anyway, it was all bullshit. There was no beam. She was just making it up with her mind.

You are trapped in you, the beam said.

Yeah, well, who isn't? she thought.

For some reason, the flock of geese was now passing back overhead, headed in the opposite direction.

That's really the problem, though, isn't it? she thought.

Yes, the beam said.

She could see Keith moving around in the kitchen.

Good old Keith. Since the incident, he had — he had not been doing well. At night, sometimes she'd hear him crying in the

133

pantry. And this week he'd been passed over at work again. People just — they didn't respect him. At the office Christmas party, everyone kept talking over him. There'd been some kind of running joke about everyone funneling the least desirable projects to Keith and Keith cluelessly accepting. He'd just sat there, fingering a poinsettia leaf that had fallen off the centerpiece. No one even seemed to notice that they were hurting his feelings.

Sweet guy. Weak guy.

Her weak, sweet guy.

This limping info?

Was dying with her, here and now.

She was going to have to be kind of a sin-eater on this one.

What she had to do was go in there, say nothing. About the limp. Be cheerful, be happy. Make the Christmas cookies. As planned. At every turn, all evening, fight the urge to tell him. Tomorrow, when, again, she felt the urge, remind herself that she had decided, here in the car, for the good of the family, not to tell him. Ever. Next day, same thing. With each passing day, the desire to tell him would diminish. And one day soon, she'd get through the whole day without even thinking of telling him.

And that would be that.

She just had to start the process.

On the passenger seat was a plastic bag. In the bag: a roll of parchment paper, a thing of sprinkles, three new cookie cutters. What she had to do now was reach over, pick up the bag, open the car door, drop one foot into the gray slush.

That, she could do.

That was something good she could actually do.

LOVE LETTER

February 22, 202_.

Dear Robbie,

Got your email, kid. Sorry for handwriting in reply. Not sure emailing is the best move, considering the topic, but, of course (you being nearly six foot now, your mother says), that's up to you, dear, although, you know: strange times.

Beautiful day here. Family of deer just now raced past and your grandmother and I, out on the deck, holding the bright blue mugs you kindly sent at Christmas, did simultaneous hip swivels as they sprang off toward Seascape and, I expect, an easy meal on the golf course there.

Forgive my use of initials in what follows. Would not wish to cause further difficulties for G., M., or J. (good folks all, we very much enjoyed meeting them when you stopped by over Easter) should this get sidetracked and read by someone other than you.

136

I think you are right regarding G. That ship has sailed. Best to let that go. M., per your explanation, does not lack proper paperwork but did know, all the while, that G. was lacking it, yes? And did nothing about that? Am not suggesting, of course, that she should have. But, putting ourselves into "their" heads (the heads of the loyalists) — as I think, these days, it is prudent to try to do — we might ask: Why didn't M. (again, according to them, to their way of thinking) do what she "should" have done, by letting someone in authority know about G.? Since being here is "a privilege and not a right." Are we or are we not (as I have grown sick of hearing) "a nation of laws"?

Even as they change the laws constantly to suit their own beliefs!

Believe me, I am as disgusted as you are with all of this.

But the world, in my (ancient) experience, sometimes moves off in a certain direction and, having moved, being so large and inscrutable, cannot be recalled to its previous, better state, and so, in this current situation, it behooves us, I would say, to think as they think, as well as we can manage, to avoid as much unpleasantness and future harm as possible.

Of course, you were writing, really, to ask

about J. Yes, am still in touch with the lawyer you mentioned. Don't honestly feel he would be much help. At this point. In his prime, he was, yes, a prince of a guy striding into a courthouse, but he is not now the man he once was. He opposed, perhaps too energetically, the DOJ review/ouster of sitting judges and endured much abuse in the press and his property was defaced and he was briefly detained and these days, from what I have heard, is mostly just puttering around his yard, keeping his views very much to himself.

Where is J. now? Do you know? State facility or fed? That may matter. I expect "they" (loyalists) would (with the power of the courts now behind them) say that although J. is a citizen, she forfeited certain rights and privileges by declining to offer the requested info on G. & M. You may recall R. & K., friends of ours, who gave you, for your fifth (sixth?) birthday, that bronze Lincoln bank? They are loyalists, still in touch, and that is the sort of logic they follow. A guy over in Aptos Village befriended a fellow at their gym and they would take runs together and so forth, and the first guy, after declining to comment on what he knew of his new friend's voting past, suddenly found he could no longer register his work vehicle (he was a florist, so this proved problematic). R. & K.'s take on this: a person is "no patriot" if he refuses to answer a "simple question" from his "own homeland government."

That is where we find ourselves.

You asked if you are supposed to stand by and watch your friend's life be ruined.

Two answers: one as a citizen, the other as a grandfather. (You have turned to me in what must be a difficult time and I am trying to be frank.)

As a citizen: I can, of course, understand why a young (intelligent, good-looking) person (perpetual delight to know, I might add) would feel that it is his duty to "do something" on behalf of his friend J.

But what, exactly?

That is the question.

When you reach a certain age, you see that time is all we have. By which I mean, moments like those springing deer this morning, and watching your mother be born, and sitting at the dining room table here waiting for the phone to ring and announce that a certain baby (you) had been born, or that day when all of us hiked out at Point Lobos. That extremely loud seal, your sister's scarf drifting down, down to that black, briny boulder, the replacement you so generously bought her in Monterey, how pleased you made her with your kindness. Those things were real. That is what (that is all) one gets. All this other stuff is real only to the extent that it interferes with those moments.

Now, you may say (I can hear you saying it and see the look on your face as you do) that this incident with J. *is* an interference. I respect that. But, as your grandfather, I beg you not to underestimate the power/ danger of this moment. Perhaps I have not yet mentioned this to you: in the early days of this thing, I wrote two letters to the editor of the local rag, one overwrought, the other comic. Neither had any effect. Those who agreed with me agreed with me; those who did not remained unpersuaded. After a third attempt was rejected, I found myself pulled over, up near the house, for no reason I could discern. The cop (nice guy, just a kid, really) asked what I did all day. Did I have any hobbies? I said no. He said: Some of us heard you like to type. I sat in my car, looking over at his large, pale arm. His face was the face of a kid. His arm, though, was the arm of a man.

How would you know about that? I said.

Have a good night, sir, he said. Stay off the computer.

Good Lord, his stupidity and bulk there in the darkness, the metallic clanking from his belt area, the palpable certainty he seemed to feel regarding his cause, a cause I cannot begin, even at this late date, to get my head around, or view from within, so to speak.

I do not want you anywhere near, or under the sway of, that sort of person, ever.

I feel here a need to address the last part of your email, which (I want to assure you) did not upset me or "hurt my feelings." No. When you reach my age, and if you are lucky enough to have a grandson like you (stellar), you will know that nothing that grandson could say could ever hurt your feelings, and, in fact, I am so touched that you thought to write me in your time of need and be so direct and even (I admit it) somewhat rough with me.

Seen in retrospect, yes: I have regrets. There was a certain critical period. I see that now. During that period, your grandmother and I were working on, every night, a jigsaw puzzle each, at that dining room table I know you know well. We were planning to have the kitchen redone, were in the midst of having the walls out there in the yard rebuilt at great expense, I was experi-

141

encing the first intimations of the dental issues I know you have heard so much (perhaps too much) about. Every night, as we sat across from each other, doing those puzzles, from the TV in the next room blared this litany of things that had never before happened, that we could never have imagined happening, that were now happening, and the only response from the TV pundits was a wry, satirical smugness that assumed, as we assumed, that those things could and would soon be undone and that all would return to normal — that some adult or adults would arrive, as they had always arrived in the past, to set things right. It did not seem (and please destroy this letter after you have read it) that someone so clownish could disrupt something so noble and time-tested and seemingly strong, something that had been with us literally every day of our lives. We had taken, in other words, a profound gift for granted. Did not know the gift was a fluke, a chimera, a wonderful accident of consensus and mutual understanding.

Because this destruction was emanating from such an inept source, who seemed (at that time) merely comically thuggish, who seemed to know so little about that which he was disrupting, and because life was going on, and because every day he/they burst through some new gate of propriety, we soon found that no genuine outrage was available to us anymore. If you'll allow me a crude metaphor (as I'm sure you, the King of Las Bromas de Fartos, will): a guy comes into a dinner party, takes a dump on the rug in the living room. The guests get excited, yell out in protest. He takes a second dump. The guests feel, Well, yelling didn't help. (While some of them applaud his audacity.) He takes a third dump, on the table, and still no one throws him out. At that point, the sky has become the limit in terms of future dumps.

So, although your grandmother and I, during this critical period, often said, you know, "Someone should arrange a march" or "Those f——ing Republican senators," we soon grew weary of hearing ourselves saying these things and, to avoid being old people emptily repeating ourselves, stopped saying those things, and did our puzzles and so forth, waiting for the election.

I'm speaking here of the third, not the fourth (of the son), which, being a total sham, didn't hurt (surprise) as much.

Post-election, doing new puzzles (mine a difficult sort of Catskills summer scene), noting those early pardons (which, by the time they were granted, we'd been well prepared to expect), and then that deluge of pardons (each making way for the next), and the celebratory verbal nonsense accompanying the pardons (to which, again, we were, by this time, somewhat inured), and the targeting of judges, and the incidents in Reno and Lowell, and the investigations into pundits, and the casting aside of even the expanded term limits, we still did not really believe that the thing was happening. Birds still burst out of the trees and so forth.

I feel I am disappointing you.

I just want to say that history, when it arrives, may not look as you expect, based on the reading of history books. Things in there are always so clear. One knows exactly what one would have done.

Your grandmother and I (and many others) would have had to be more extreme people than we were, during that critical period, to have done whatever it was we should have been doing. Our lives had not prepared us for extremity, to mobilize or be as focused and energized as I can see, in retrospect, we would have needed to be. We were not prepared to drop everything in defense of a system that was, to us, like oxygen: used constantly, never noted. We were spoiled, I think I am trying to say. As were those on the other side: willing to tear it all down because they had been so thoroughly nourished by the vacuous plenty in which we all lived, a bountiful condition that allowed people to thrive and opine and swagger around like kings and queens while remaining ignorant of their own history.

What would you have had me do? What would you have done? I know what you will say: you would have fought. But how? How would you have fought? Would you have called your senator? (In those days, you could still, at least, record your feeble message on a senator's answering machine without reprisal, but you might as well have been singing or whistling or passing wind into it for all the good it did.) Well, we did that. We called, we wrote letters. Would you have given money to certain people running for office? We did that as well. Would you have marched? For some reason, there were suddenly no marches. Organized a march? Then and now, I did not and do not know how to arrange a march. I was still working full-time. This dental thing had just begun. That rather occupies the mind. You know where we live. Would you have had me drive down to Watsonville and harangue the officials there? They were all in agreement with us. At that time. Would you have armed yourself? I would not and will not, and I do not believe you would either. I hope not. By that, all is lost.

Let me, at the end, return to the beginning, and be blunt: I advise and implore you to stay out of this business with J. Your involvement will not help (especially if you don't know where they have taken her, fed or state) and may, in fact, hurt. I hope I do not offend if I here use the phrase "empty gesture." Not only will J.'s situation be made worse, so might those of your mother, father, sister, grandmother, grandfather, etc. Part of the complication here is that you are not alone in this.

I want you well. I want you someday to be an old fart yourself, writing a (too) long letter to a (beloved) grandson. In this world, we speak much of courage and not, I feel, enough about discretion, about caution. I know how that will sound to you. Let it be. I have lived this long and have the right.

It occurs to me only now that you and J. may have been more than just friends.

That, if the case, would, I know (must) complicate the matter.

I had, last night, a vivid dream of those days, of that critical, pre-election period. I was sitting across from your grandmother, her at work on her puzzle (puppies and kittens), me on mine (gnomes in trees), and suddenly we saw, in a flash, things as they were, that is, we realized that this was the critical moment. We looked at each other across the table with such freshness, if I may say it that way, such love for each other and for our country, the country in which we had lived our whole lives, the many roads, hills, lakes, malls, byways, villages we had known and moved about and around so freely.

How precious and lovely it all seemed.

Your grandmother stood, with that decisiveness I know you know.

"Let us think of what we must do," she said.

Then I woke. There in bed, I felt, for a brief instant, that it was *that* time again and not *this* time. Lying there, I found myself wondering, for the first time in a long while, not "What should I have done?" but "What might I yet do?"

I came back to myself, gradually. It was sad. A sad moment. To be, once again, in a time and place where action was not possible.

I wish with all my heart that we could have passed it all on to you intact. I do. That is, now, not to be. That regret I will take to my grave. Wisdom, now, amounts to making such intelligent accommodations as we can. I am not saying stick your head in the sand. J. made a choice. She could have told all, regarding G. and M. She did not. I respect that. And yet. No one is calling on you to do anything. You are, in my view, doing much good simply by rising in the morning, being as present as possible, keeping sanity alive in the world, so that, someday, when (if) this thing passes, the country may find its way back to normalcy, with your help and the help of those like you.

But please know that I understand how hard it must be to stay silent and inactive if, in fact, J. was more than just a friend. She is a lovely person and I recall her crossing our yard with her particular grace and brio, swinging your car keys on that long chain, her dog (Whiskey?) trotting along beside her. It is true, as you say: we have no idea what is going on with her, in this new world of ours. And that must, yes, of course, weigh heavily on one's mind, especially if that relationship was intimate, and might well (how could it not?) create a feeling that one should act.

I feel I have made my preference clear, above. I say what follows not to encourage.

We have money (not much, but some) set aside. Should push come to shove. I am finding it hard to advise you. I do not wish to disappoint. Nor lead you astray. With age, one becomes cautious. It is a curse. We love you so much. Please let us know what you are inclined to do, as we find that this (you) is all that we now can think of.

With love, much love, more than you can know,

GPa.

A Thing at Work

Genevieve Turner stepped back into the break room.

Yep, there were her keys, on top of the microwave.

Also in there now (ugh): Brenda.

Gen braced for the onslaught.

Here it came.

Gosh, wow, Brenda said, it seems crazy that they watched your time card so close and yet look at all these coffee thingies on the counter a person could just take and who'd ever know? Were those coffee thingies cheap? She doubted it! Why not make people write it down whenever they put in a fresh coffee thingie? Ever heard of cost control? Not that anybody here would sink so low. As to steal coffee. They got paid good. Pretty good. Some better than others. Ha! But same with the paper towels on top of the fridge, though: why not just hang a sign up there saying, PLEASE TAKE?

Brenda was small, round, sweet, standing there in one of those too-short blouses she was always tugging down over her toddler-esque belly: *elfin,* if you were feeling generous.

Greggie and Bethie were both, sadly, yeah, living with her now, again, in her same old crappo two-bedroom, she said. Although how cool was that, to have your two grown kiddos so close at hand? Although how about cooking something once in a while, dudes? Even a grilled cheese once a week would be the bomb. Lately she'd been taking the bus to work, because the car was in that frigging rip-off of a shop again, yeah, so soon as she got home she'd have to fry something up for her two little deadbeats while they sat on the couch looking over at her like (and here she made a deadbeat face: dropping her jaw, crossing her eyes).

Gen glanced longingly back at the hallway.

Brenda had more to share.

Well, the people you loved in this world were all that mattered. That's what she thought, anyway. Some people didn't get that. She could do with a little less stupid, though! Like, last week, she'd had to stay until midnight, unbinding eight hundred frigging reports. Because *a certain dodo* hadn't liked Figure 6b. Did it ever occur to him to maybe order pizza for the lady (her) staying late, the worker bee, the big nobody? Ha. She'd sat there cross-legged on that thin carpet they had in the copy room over that hard cement floor, unbinding, totally starving, while the *certain dodo* was over at his kid's cello recital, and after that they'd probably all gone for a big feed somewhere nice, unlike her, who, all she'd had was three bags of chips for dinner from the vending machine in the frigging atrium and that was it. *Bon appétit,* right?

Tim Rupp stepped in. The *certain dodo.* Yikes. Had Tim heard all that?

Brenda blushed, did a strange little bow, backed out.

"Whoa," Gen said to Tim in an undertone, meaning, That Brenda, right? What a hoot.

Expecting a look of collegial commiseration, she instead found herself receiving a judgment-laced sadness-wince.

"Well," Tim said. "She's had a tough row to hoe."

What? Oh, great. Now Tim saw her, Gen, as the snob who enjoyed good wines and custom mustards and kicking the white-trash lady when she was down? The shallow elitist, bashing the trailer gal?

What could she say to make this right?

Tim, just so you know? I only said "Whoa"

because, before you came in, Brenda had been speaking rather disrespectfully about you, and the reason I didn't confront her was because I was trying to be compassionate, precisely because she's had a rough hoe to row, or however you just now put it.

Too much.

Plus, Brenda might hear it from her office.

Anyway, Tim was gone. It was just her in here. And Tim's coffee cup, spinning around on that glass plate, giving off sparks, because the genius didn't know you couldn't put a cup with a metal rim in a microwave.

Back in her office, Brenda was manically wiping her keyboard with a Kleenex. Ah, jeez, she thought, did I just now throw the kids under the bus? By calling them "deadbeats"? No, I wouldn't do that. That's not how I am. Plus, anyways, they *are* deadbeats. Ha. Whatever, they can take it, they're not made of sugar, they won't melt. Also, probably shouldn't have said that thing about stealing coffee. Because now Gen might think I actually have done that.

Which, in fact, she had been doing that, since the day she came back to work here two months ago after the little issue with the bounced checks and the, uh, stint, or stent, of jail time or whatever, but you know what? Coffee was ten bucks a *can*. Paper towels were seven bucks a *pack*. It helped! Maybe, for some people, ten bucks was nothing, but it wasn't nothing for her. If only they'd leave some steaks and veggies and gas money and rent money out where she could get at it. Ha ha. No: she was no thief. I mean, she was but she wasn't. Okay, she was. Ha. The thing about it was, there was a shit ton of stealing going on around here *all the time.* Mike G. called his fiancée in England on the office phone *every day.* Gen went on long lunches with Ed Maxx from Kodak and Brenda knew where (Olive Garden) and where they went after (Riverside Marriott) because she made the frigging reservations. Gen would breeze back in around four, still buzzed, just boinked, hand Brenda her leftovers in a wadded-up tinfoil swan. Did Gen then turn right around and bill those hours to Kodak? With a straight face? *Yeah,* she did! Was that stealing? Hey, that was *big-time* stealing.

Nine coffee pouches a month was, like, twenty bucks. Twenty bucks was nothing. Power to the people, right on. Plus, she had carpal tunnel. Every word she typed was one word closer to never being able to type again and having to go back to cleaning condos for Manny. And Manny was creepy. The things you had to clean in those Section 8 crapholes! Two hundred literal raw chicken gizzards off a kitchen floor. A whole closet full of upside-down cupcakes. Who'd turned them upside down like that? And why? Was Manny the kind of boss who gave you gloves? No, he was the kind of boss who made you walk to Walmart to buy your frigging own.

The way to steal a coffee pouch was: grab one, stroll back to your office holding it down by your hip. Once in your office, plop in purse. If, out in the hall, somebody saw you? Look down all of a sudden at the coffee thingie, go, "Ah jeez, senile much?," then go back to break room, toss coffee thingie on counter, go, "Criminy, I'd lose my head if it wasn't hooked on." Or, if nobody was around, bring your purse right into the break room. *Voilà*. Ka-ching. Three bucks.

Six bucks, nine bucks, whatever.

Paper towels, same deal, only harder, because bigger. Tuck a roll under each arm, haul balls down the long hall, heart beating like crazy because if somebody saw you, you couldn't just go, "Ah jeez, senile much?" because you'd have to be pretty dang senile for real not to notice a paper towel roll under each of your arms, plus sometimes you could do two per arm, total of four, sticking out from both armpits.

Last night this guy on the bus had looked over at her like: Uh, what's with the paper towels, lady? And she'd gone, in her mind: Hey, loser, I stopped by CVS on my way to the bus, up yours, idiot, and by the way, the reason they're not in a bag is, I told the CVS kid no thanks, because of the environment, unlike you, who just now dropped your frigging gum wrapper on the floor, slob.

No, she loved people. People were great. Even that dolt on the bus. He'd probably given her that cranky look because he'd had a bad day, which, given that ugly mug? No surprise there. Who'd marry that? Nah, even ugly folks got married. They married other uglies. It all worked out. Plus, she herself wasn't married. At the moment. She'd been married once. To Norbert. Norb the Orb. That ugly guy on the bus had probably never been married at all. Too ugly. Poor dope. Once the cranky look faded off that dweeb's judgmental puss, he'd gone back to staring out the window, all sad now, like he was thinking back to when he was in grade school and all of life was still ahead of him and he hadn't yet realized how ugly he was. Or maybe he only got ugly later, gradually, in high school. He'd stand at the mirror before gym class, going: What the what? Is my face ever going back to regular?

But no, it wasn't.

After dark the bus windows turned into mirrors. She'd sat there looking at that sad look on the guy's ugly mug being reflected in the mirror the window had just become. Looking at his reflection, she'd seen her reflection, and guess what? Same sad look.

Ah, jeez, why sad, what am I sad about? she'd thought. Nothing, nothing, I'm happy, lucky, going home to two great kids. Out of jail and back to work. With four rolls of paper towels I didn't even pay for. And a thingie of coffee in the old purserino.

Then the face of hers she saw in the bus window was: ornery.

Gen swiveled her chair to stretch her legs. Wow, her legs were, she had to say, gloriously long. She was like some kind of gorgeous thoroughbred. If she said so herself. Which she did. Got it? Flaunt it.

Although she did not feel at peace. Why not? Think it through.

Well, Ed had just texted again. Third time today. Could they meet at Seneca Park? Just to talk? An hour without her seemed like a year, he'd said. All morning he'd been dreaming of the smell of her, the taste of her, the feel of himself inside her.

It was wrong but felt so right.

Had they really done it on the pitcher's mound at Frontier Field in the dead of winter? Check. Had she really given him a hand job in the Wendy's drive-through? Roger that. It had all been for fun. And he was fun. Hung like a horse, quite the kisser. Said all the right things. After this, seriously? Faithful forever. To Rob. Unless someone else awesome came along. What was she, dead? Rob was great, Rob was thoughtful, Rob was sweet. But she *had* Rob. What she'd found out about herself, six months into their marriage, was that what she loved (what she lived for, actually) was: getting someone new to want her. There was nothing like it. Sue her, she wanted to live. She and Rob had an open thing. Rob was cool with it. She, yes, invoked the open thing somewhat more often than Rob. Who, so far, had never once invoked it.

But that wasn't it.

It was this thing with Brenda. Tim might be down in his office right now, thinking less of her. Believing that she'd been agreeing with Brenda's negative yammering about him. Why did she care? Well, she did. That's just how she was. Responsible. Good team player. Tim was, after all, their boss.

Their "boss."

Hard to believe that shrimp was anybody's "boss."

Ugh, this was going to ruin her whole day if she didn't take care of it.

She'd go down there, bring up the topic of Brenda, giving Tim a chance to say, Yeah, you know, I heard something kind of weird just now, back in the break room. Then she'd confess. Confess that Brenda had been shit-talking him. While she, Gen, very much disapproving of that kind of talk, had stood there helplessly trapped by her own politeness.

She strode down to Tim's office and dropped into his wobbly guest chair with a soldierly familiarity.

"That Brenda, wow," she said. "I just love her. What a wild card. Sort of hard to break away from, you know? Once she gets going. She just talks and talks and says the rudest, most inexplicable things. I find myself literally avoiding the break room if she's in there. Which is sad. Because I know she's had some issues. But still, wow."

Tim pulled the front-end loader out of his fleet of toy trucks and rolled it over to some pencils he'd apparently rubber-banded together to, she guessed, represent some sort of payload. What was he, six? The loader, scooping up the pencil-bundle, knocked it off the cliff that was the desk.

Bending to retrieve it, he looked up at her, like: And?

This was, she saw, possibly, a blunder. Apparently, Tim hadn't even heard Brenda shit-talking him. And now she was making it worse, by reinforcing Tim's sense of her, Gen, as a snob who'd made the long stroll down here merely to underscore how laughable she found lowly Brenda.

Oh, the hell with it, she was just going to say it, to get it off her mind, so she could go back to work.

"Listen," she said. "I hate doing this? But Brenda, just now, in the break room? Called you a 'dodo.' Honestly, my jaw dropped. I was so shocked, I couldn't respond. And I didn't want you thinking I was on board with that. If, you know, you heard it."

"A dodo," Tim said, seeming more amused by the word choice than offended by the insult.

What a strange, off-focus little person.

"Well, it's a free country," he said. "My guess is, she probably says things like that because she feels insecure. What with the jail situation and all? Anyway, I don't see any need for us to be running around turning each other in, you know?"

What? So now she was a narc? An over-involved tattletale casting shit on perfect, saintly Brenda? And was supposed to meekly walk out of here, chastened, knowing all she knew about Saint Brenda, i.e., that this name-calling tendency of hers was only the tip of the frigging iceberg?

No, sorry, she literally couldn't do it.

Then it occurred to her why she'd really come in here. Or, rather, a way occurred to her by which she could rebut Tim's facile dismissal of her, i.e., by which she could eradicate Tim's sense of her as someone who'd come in here just to rat out someone for calling him a dodo, when, in fact, what she'd really come in here for was —

Ah, yes.

There it was.

"Tim," she said. "Something's been going on around here. For a long time now. I don't know if you're aware of it. Apparently not."

That got his attention.

She took out her phone, put it on the desk, hit Play.

The video showed Brenda stepping into the break room, casting a surreptitious glance around, stuffing one, two, three coffee bags into her purse. Then a cut and she was waddling down the main hallway,

161

whistling, a roll of paper towels under each arm. Then another cut and she was fleeing the supply closet, hands full of Sharpies, like a drunk in a silent film who'd broken into a cigar store.

"Why were you even taking these?" Tim said.

What an offensive question! Would he have asked that of a man? Come on, it was hilarious! This stout middle-aged chick stealing from work in plain sight? Last night, she and Rob had watched the new edit like six times, with Byron, her godly little stepson, their one-kid Morality Commission.

"I'm not sure that's nice, Mom," Byron had said. "Seems kind of harsh."

"Well, she is *stealing,* bud," Rob had said cheerfully.

Rob was crazy about her. Always took her side. In everything.

"That doesn't mean we have to make fun of her," Byron said.

"We don't have to," she said.

"We just like to," Rob said.

And Byron had slunk off to do his origami. Odd little duck.

Tim was gazing meditatively out the window. As if deciding what to do. Although, if she knew Tim, he was just pretending to be deciding. So that she'd leave, so he could get back to playing with his toys.

"Tim, she's *stealing*," she said. "She's a *thief*. I just thought you should know. Being the boss and all. No offense."

They both sat there stiffly as she emailed him the video.

Gen, Gen, Tim thought as she left, why not mind your own business for once?

Gen was a tall, willowy, somewhat sexy, if you were into a certain aging-hippie vibe, show-off, always bustling around the office, coffee in hand, asking if everyone was doing great, saying she was stoked, that it felt like they were doing some truly positive things for the world, sometimes singing out, "Big things happening!" in this Ethel Merman voice, or else you'd find her pruning the peace lily near reception.

"Pretty expensive gardener," he'd said once.

"Don't worry, Captain Nervous," she'd replied. "I'm billing Xerox."

He felt intimidated by Gen, he had to admit it. She was taller than him, for one thing. Sometimes she'd throw one long arm over his shoulders while fondly looking down at him, like she was the guy and he was the girl. It was weird. Interesting. Kind of troubling. Plus, he only had his bachelor's, in Recreational Facility Design Management, whereas Gen had a master's in biology and her parents had both been astrophysicists, whereas his mom had been a tollbooth attendant and his dad also a tollbooth attendant, who'd left them when Tim was six and gone to Nevada to be a tollbooth attendant there, while Mom continued to work at the same old tollbooth just outside Schenectady.

Anyway, wow: Brenda was stealing.

Brenda, already on thin ice, was stealing.

Brenda was slow. Brenda was sloppy. Last time he'd given her a typing job, she'd missed three whole pages of changes and he'd had to point it out, trying, because Brenda was touchy, not to say, you know, "How the heck does a person miss three heavily-edited-in-red pages of changes?" but, rather, "Ha ha, not to be picky, but seems like these pages here might benefit from another pass, if you would?" And Brenda had gone, "Ah jeez, stupid much? Sorry, hon, sorry." To which, to be polite, he'd had to say, "Well, we all make mistakes," then offer up an example of a mistake he'd recently made, which was, while up on a ladder at the cottage, he'd gotten stung in the face by four bees at once and, falling off the ladder, had taken the gutter down with him, then landed on the new rabbit hutch, which, luckily, didn't yet have any rabbits in it.

Brenda had pronounced him a "stand-up laddie" (in a bad Irish brogue) and advised him that, when on a ladder, a person should always have a spotter, then strolled away, and he hadn't gotten his (very simple) corrections back until nearly three hours later, because she'd had to run home to let her grown son into the apartment, because he'd again left his keys behind somewhere, because he had Post-Traumatic Forgetfulness Tendency (PTFT), whatever that was, and even then half the corrections hadn't been made, and, pointing this out, he'd let the slightest hint of irritation creep into his voice, and Brenda's eyes had teared up and she'd said she honestly did not know what was up with her lately and really appreciated how patient he, Tim, always was with her, because a lot of people around here were *not* patient with her, not at all, *au contraire,* which she found hurtful, due to her recent difficulties, by which she meant having been in the county slammer down on Glass Street for three months for bouncing a shit ton of checks, and then she'd wiped her eyes with the hem of her blouse, bending her face down to the hem so her belly wouldn't show, and then her glasses fell off the top of her head and, going to pick them up, she booted them under his desk, then burst into tears and fled out of his office a lot faster than you'd expect a gal like her to be able to flee, so he'd had to get down on all fours and retrieve Brenda's glasses and take them down to her, only to find her sitting in her office in the dark, and she'd just held out her hand for the glasses, as if she was so distraught that even saying thanks would cause a new round of weeping.

That was Brenda.

Nice lady, lots of issues, okay, but come on.

This was a place of work.

Here she came now. On break, walking past his window. Wearing that coat. Weird coat. Of the type that had been called, he believed, back in the day, a "car coat." Big furry thing. Like a shepherd might wear. Mom used to have one. Or maybe it was Dad's? And she'd just started wearing it? After Dad left. Something about that coat had always bothered him. Why would someone so pretty agree to look so goofy? He had a memory of Mom going out the door in that coat. Into a blizzard. For groceries. Leaving him alone in the apartment. For the first time. Because Dad had taken the car. To Nevada. Their only car. That asshole. Mom was fallen in that way. She, who he adored, was fallen. She should have been sitting on a throne, going to fancy balls, being waited on hand and foot. But no. She was trudging down the block in a blizzard, looking like a tiny discouraged prospector.

Always, during that period, she'd been the only single mother at his school events. She'd come in late, sit at the back of the room, smiling eagerly. When someone approached, she'd freeze up, struggle to get through her thought, blush, try to back out of it with a string of halting banalities while casting a series of alarmed glances over at him to see if she was proving an embarrassment to him, her star, her little achiever, the one good thing left in her life.

There'd been this one night when the person to whom she'd been speaking, a man, wearing his hat inside for some reason, had — well, Tim understood now that the man had been flirting with her. She was pretty, if poor, and coming there alone made her vulnerable to that sort of thing. She didn't mean "reactionary," the man said, in this jolly, haughty voice; she must mean "reactive." Unless she meant to say that the kids' gym teacher was some sort of anti-reformist? Had that been her intention? Then he and a couple other creeps stood there having a big hoot about it.

Did that bastard think he was being funny? Helpful? To this nice lady? Who found herself in a great, lonely struggle? Both her parents were dead; she literally had nowhere to go. And had a kid. Him. Tim. Mr. Hat-On-Indoors could have been nice. Could have been kind. But he had her on the ropes and was going to land a few punches. What possessed a person?

That son of a bitch, whoever he was, would be nearly eighty now. If still alive. How satisfying it would be to track him down in whatever old folks' home he was in, probably pedantically torturing the other mortified residents, stride up to him at dinner, snatch away his meal, sarcastically apologize for being "reactionary."

And all the old people would stand up and creakily applaud.

Good old Mom. Dead for nine years now. He hoped, wherever she was, she knew how much he'd loved her. Such a sweetie. All she'd ever needed was one break. One kind person in her corner. For things, just once, to go her way. But no. She kept getting kicked. Over and over. By whoever felt like it. If you kicked someone like that, you were just one more person on the list of the many people who'd kicked her. Nobody would ever blame you. Whereas if you stood up for someone like that, you risked becoming — well, you risked becoming one of them.

But things were different now.

Now he had the power.

Here's what we're going to do, he thought.

And already it was making him happy.

He wouldn't fire Brenda. No. He'd call her down, show her the video, gently explain that she wasn't in trouble. But the stealing had to stop. Right? Did that seem fair? He understood why she might have been inclined to do that. He wasn't judging her. Maybe they could work on this thing together? If she was short on cash, he'd find her some extra hours. It could be their little secret.

To hell with it.

Sometimes you had to be decent.

Ten minutes later, Brenda stumbled out of Tim's office, so mad she lurched off to one side and clunked into the wall before righting herself.

You dumb tall slut, she thought. This is what you do? Narc me out? Me, the one who does all your shitwork, you boobless snooty tall drink of water? Take secret mov-

169

ies of me? Blow me, sister. Super rude, go fuck yourself.

The bullshit a person had to put up with! She worked longer hours than any of them and made like ten times less and didn't get to lounge around discussing shit such as new clients and Lessons Learned and hadn't gotten to make a spaceship out of Legos that time in Team Building but just had to sit there in her dungeon all day like a good robot and type and type while everyone else sat out there laughing and yapping about Proactive Complaint Assessment and then they all left work early to go to a bar or some such shit and came in hungover and late the next morning to put in, like, ten minutes of work before sneaking out for lunch and a fuck.

Speaking of which.

Ha!

She pulled open a file drawer.

They just dumped their stupid typing jobs on the desk of the nameless blob, her, then rode her all day until she got it done, then pissed and moaned about even the smallest mistake, then went out to lunch while she skipped lunch or, if she did get lunch, it was just an apple and a slice of cheese in a plastic sack from home that she lugged up to that picnic table on top of that weird little man-made hill looking down on the utility shed, and even then she never got her whole hour because some entitled jerk would suddenly be standing at the bottom of the hill, yelling up that she was the roadblock, she was the one holding everything up, get down here, come down here right away, Brenda, Jesus! And down that steep hill she'd come at a high rate of speed, trying not to take a tumble like that one time when she'd had on the little heels she'd started wearing to at least try to look nice, and did that person, Chaz or Donald or Kirk or whoever, as she hit that bottom part of the hill that was somehow both steep and mushy, put out his hand, to help her down, like a gentleman? No! He was already heading back across the parking lot, as if she were some stray lazy cow being led back to the herd, not turning around to chat or be nice, not holding the door open for her but just letting it glide shut in her face.

Now she had a nice little pile. Of reservation records. From the Marriott. And another pile, of Gen's time sheets. Gen had been at the Marriott from eleven a.m. until four p.m. on May 9th. For example. And billed Kodak for the whole day. And there were, like, twelve more fricking examples.

Checkmate, glamour-puss. I am taking

exactly no more of your shit.

Tim came back from lunch to find a rubber-banded file folder on his chair.

Inside was a pile of receipts from the Marriott, with a hand-scrawled note stapled to the top of it: "They go HERE to F***!"

Jeez.

He sat down, read through it.

Wait, what? Gen was sneaking away? With Ed Maxx? On Kodak's dime? Wow. Why? Ed was old. Ed was small, smaller, even, than him, Tim. And poor Rob. Gen's husband. Nice guy. Crazy about Gen. Sent her roses every Monday, after twelve years of marriage. Last Monday, he'd hired an opera student from the university to bring the roses down. The kid had been led singing down to Gen's office by Kiley, the receptionist, who'd kept bowing to the people in the offices they passed, as if she were the one doing the singing.

He laid the receipts and time sheets out. Spent a few minutes calculating the approximate amount Kodak had been unfairly billed (around $9,000 (!)). Then typed up a summary sheet, printed it, highlighted the final figure in yellow, called Gen down.

At first, she denied it. Then burst into tears. He felt bad. About the crying. He

172

didn't care, he told her, what she did in her private life, but she couldn't do it on company time. Did she see that? Did she agree?

"Who gave you these?" she said.

"I honestly don't know," he said. "They were just on my chair. And I'm not sure that's really the —"

"Was it Brenda?" she said. "Was it that fucking Brenda?"

Well, it made sense. Brenda was the only one with access to —

"Bitch!" Gen said.

"Whoa," he said.

"We'll see about this," she said, getting up, sending the guest chair flying.

"I'm not firing you," he said.

"No shit!" she yelled back over her shoulder.

Within the hour he got a call from Ed Maxx. There was a big job coming down the pike, Ed said. Huge job, one of those legendary Kodak jobs, fat charge numbers for everybody, multiyear duration. He'd been discussing it, for a while now, with Gen. In various private, off-site strategy meetings they'd been holding. Which explained, in case there was any question about it, some hours Gen had billed. To

Kodak. He, as the Kodak rep, was hereby, or forthwith, sanctioning those charges. All of them. There was nothing funny going on, by the way, despite certain, sexist, rumors. They sometimes would, yes, true, book a room at the Marriott, but that was in order to access certain spreadsheets, on the, you know, internet, because the wireless at the Olive Garden was crap.

Tim found himself so awed by the brazenness of the lie that he couldn't summon up the words to indicate that he would pretend to accept it for the sake of politeness.

"What is it?" he finally stammered out. "What's the big project?"

"I'm not at liberty to say," Ed said. "At this time. Soon, it will be announced. By me. Or another. For now, it's secret. Another thing, if I may, since I've got you? I've been hearing some disturbing rumors. Regarding stealing. Some stealing you've got going on over there? This is something that concerns me, obviously, as your client. Your biggest client, if I'm not mistaken. If it means, as I suppose it does, increased costs for us, for Kodak. Can I trust that you'll take care of this, Tim? By getting rid of the person doing the stealing, i.e., the thief, whoever she may be? Or he? Or she? Asap?"

Ha, wow.

174

Well played, Gen. Now he had to fire Brenda. He did. Ed Maxx was a killer. He had to let Brenda go. Had to release Brenda, so she could approach alternative prospective employers to identify possible growth opportunities more consistent with her unique skill set and interests.

He had kids. He had a mortgage.

This was the real world.

To his earlier self, the self who'd sat in this very chair, patting himself on the back for being willing to step up for Brenda, he —

Well, that had been admirable. He admired that. He did. But things changed, and when they changed, a good leader had to —

Crap, shit.

He called Liz. To get her input. Liz was his rock. A total realist. She always knew the right thing to do, for his career, for their family.

He knew what he needed her to say and was pretty sure she'd say it.

He told her everything.

"Oh," she said. "That lady has to go."

"I guess so," he said.

"No, for sure," she said. "Which one is she again?"

"The short one," he said. "Sort of meek, obsequious? Maybe, uh, a bit chubby? The one who, at the Christmas party, said you were so pretty she could hardly stand to look at you?"

"Well, but still," Liz said.

He tried to soften the blow by saying what a pleasure it had been to get to know her, how much he'd miss seeing her every day, how sorry he was that it had come to this. Brenda was having none of it. She sat there like one of the working-class ladies of his childhood, bitter fighters with bright red faces, emanating a savage scary blankness that he understood to mean: Fuck you, you are not forgiven.

Not forgiven for what, though? he thought. Finding out you were a thief? When you were? Firing you? For stealing? After we were nice enough to hire you back the minute you got out of jail?

Come on.

"She steals too," Brenda said softly. "When she goes on dates with Ed and charges Kodak."

Then there was this long silence.

There was nothing he could say that wouldn't get him in deeper trouble with Ed Maxx if Brenda somehow decided to escalate things here, which, knowing her, she would.

Who wouldn't? In her position?

He would.

It was kind of a crock of shit.

But now he had to wait her out.

It would be easy enough. Beneath all the bluster, she was a timid soul. Any minute now she'd start yapping.

Down the hall in the kitchen someone slammed the microwave door shut, swore, pulled it open, slammed it shut again.

Well, Brenda finally said, on the bright side, now at least she'd get to spend more time with the kiddos. Although their place was pretty small. Just had the one bathroom. Once, when Greggie had gone in there for one of his marathon sessions? Beth had put her jam box in a lawn chair outside the bathroom door and started blasting in the disco. Which, the funny part was, Greggie actually loved disco. So that had backfired big-time on Bethie, who'd had to stiff-leg it over to the Sunoco. Which, luckily, they knew the manager over there.

He found himself forming his vehicles into a line and parading them past the desk lamp by applying a steady pressure to the last vehicle, the ice cream truck, easing off whenever the line started to buckle. Then realized he was being disrespectful. And stopped.

Finally Brenda stood, thanked him for

177

everything, shook his hand, and left.

Oh God, fired, embarrassing, she thought, fleeing down the main hall.

Why had she told him that crap about their bathroom?

What a note to end on.

She hoped she didn't run into anybody on the way out. She'd assumed everybody knew. All along. About the stealing. The borrowing. Whatever. She hadn't ever tried to hide it. Much. She assumed they all knew but nobody minded. That they all, like, blessed it. Because she was so nice. And sort of, you know, poor or whatever.

But no. They didn't. They didn't bless it.

No way. *Au contraire.*

Now she was fired.

She could just hear the kids.

Bren, fired, God, what'd you do? Bethie would say.

What'd you do this time, Bren? Greggie would say.

Get a job yourselves, dunces, she thought sharply. Then you can talk. And stop calling me Bren. I'm your mom.

Then felt bad. They were tender. Tender little noodles. She always just let them say their shit. They didn't mean any of it. Like when Greggie called her stubby little arms her "*T. rex* arms." He didn't mean it. It was his way of saying he loved her. Then he'd do the roar and she'd whack him with a couch cushion or stab him with a plastic knife and he'd pretend to be a *T. rex,* dying.

Yeah, they had their fun.

She had to figure out her next move. Manny, if he'd have her. Ugh, those green smocks he made you buy and wear. Did she have hers still? No, she'd made a big show of burning it on the grill after this place had hired her back.

Rent was coming up. Sergei, their landlord, was a toughie. With three toughie sons. They'd tossed Gordon off a landing, breaking his leg, then run down there and taken turns stomping on it, chanting the amount they figured Gordon still owed them.

Plus she had to pay the shop for the car.

Stupidhead, she thought.

She just really hurt my feelings, she thought back.

Boo-hoo, she thought.

I thought she was my friend, she thought back.

Your friend just kicked your ass, she thought. Gen 1, You 0. Right? Right?

I know it, shut up, I tried my best, she thought back.

Did you? she thought. Did you, though?

Ah, fuck Gen. And the horse she rode in on. She'd get her revenge. Someday. She would. Someday Gen and all the other fancy-pantsers would eat shit. She'd stand over them yelling as they typed. She'd make them eat lunch in a pen with the hogs. Please, Brenda, let us out, they'd say in their fruity college voices. Sorry, no, she'd say, I'm going to the spa, it's my spa day. They'd be like: Fair enough, we used to love the spa back in the olden times, before the revolution.

But you stole, right, you stole? the mean gal said in her head. So stop right there. Stop making excuses. Just stop right there and admit you stole.

That was no mean gal, that was Pop.

Pop, I stole and now I'm fired, she said.

I know it, Pop said.

Pop wanted to comfort her but was embarrassed to be the father of the lady who'd gotten fired for cause.

Then he did. Comfort her. By awkwardly patting her head in a way that felt kind of like comfort and kind of like he was rapping her on the head with his one big knuckle for being so stupid as to steal from her place of work.

Fuck 'em, Bren, Pop said. You're worth the lot of them.

This time of day the buses ran every three hours. She'd be sitting on that cracked bench in the sun forever. Did she have change for a Coke? No, and all her cards were full.

Ugh, here was Kiley, at reception, eyes cast down. Kiley knew. She must know. They all knew. Or would know soon enough.

Poor Brenda, they'd be saying in the break room.

She was so *weird,* Kylie would say.

Spare me, you glam little empty-headed scarecrow, Brenda thought. I got zits older than you.

Ah, come on. Kiley was nice. Nice enough. Just a baby, really.

"So long, kiddo," Brenda said.

"Good luck with everything," Kiley said.

"I'm going to need it," Brenda said.

Uh, yeah you are, Kiley thought as Brenda went out. Wow, not only does the older lady, like a grandma, get fired, now she has to take a bus home? Harsh. Anyway, how do you? Take a bus? She had no idea. And no plan of finding out! Having had the Prius ever since she got her license. (Thanks, Dad, thanks, Bridget!)

Why were some old people so dumb? As to get fired? Yet sweet? Who could get that old and still not know the basic stuff about how to do stuff? That's just how it was. Probably even back in caveman times there'd been smart cavepeople and dopey old sweet ones gazing over sad-eyed at the smart ones as the smart ones chewed on some big old leg of meat while looking back at the dumb ones like: Sucks for you.

Brenda struggled over the little berm at the edge of their parking lot and started off toward the TGIF, then paused to wipe her eyes with one sleeve of that nutty big coat. What? Crying? Standing there crying? In front of the TGIF?

Oh, honey.

For a second she felt protective of Brenda, who was, after all, one of theirs.

Or had been.

Until just now.

First thing next morning Gen stuck her head into Tim's office.

"Sorry all that had to happen," she said. "Can I sit?"

"Sure," he said warily.

She'd broken things off with Ed, she said. There had never been any big forthcoming project; that was just something they'd cooked up between the two of them. When she broke it off, he went a little nuts and

182

proposed to her, and when she turned him down, he called Rob, and told Rob all, and Rob, in spite of the fact that they had an open thing going on, went ballistic, and at one point last night had literally been up on the roof screaming. Then Ed, crazy Ed, had called at two a.m. and said he'd shaved his head and was thinking of quitting Kodak and moving up to Alaska. Did she want to come? He'd already bought her some top-rated mittens.

Anyway, they were okay now, they were all okay, they were working it out.

Then she thanked Tim for "calling her on her shit" and elevating her into a "state of higher honesty," which was causing good things to happen, even at home, especially at home, even in terms of the you-know-what, with Rob, which, weirdly, had never been better, or lasted longer, or been more in earnest, if she could put it that way, based, anyhow, on (late, late) last night, after he came down off the roof, which: wow.

Lady, who are you? he thought. How is it that you feel so comfortable telling me all of this? Why are you not mortified? Where do you get your insane confidence?

She knew she'd been a pain in the ass to him in the past, she said, and she'd done some real soul-searching and could see that a lot of this was due to the insecurity of being a woman in a working world dominated by men, and also some stuff from her childhood, with her mom, who was always denying her use of the superior telescope, but anyway, she wanted Tim to know that she'd resolved to try to be more helpful to him in the future, for real. She'd brought him this truck, this little garbage truck, to symbolize, well, her cleaning up her act, or whatever.

She put the little garbage truck down on the desk, so he could see how cool it was. See? The tiny bag of fake garbage on the back popped right out.

Then she rolled the truck over to him and he caught it.

SPARROW

She was small and slight and her eyes were dark beads on either side of a beaklike nose. She moved quickly, head down, as if, we sometimes joked, scanning for seeds. She had a way of seeming to dart from place to place. She had a way, too, of saying the most predictable things. When a truck went off the road in front of the little store where she worked, she said, "That's too bad. I hope no one was hurt." When it started to rain, whether drizzling or pouring, she'd say, "It's raining cats and dogs." When someone said the sandwich she was eating looked good, she'd say, "It's a good sandwich." If someone said the sandwich didn't look good, she'd say, "Yeah, not great."

If you found yourself in a car in which she was riding and someone suggested rolling down a window, she'd say, "Some fresh air." Or you'd pass a guy riding a horse and she'd say, "A horse." If someone, goading her slightly, asked, "You like horses?" she might say, "Well, they are pretty," and if that person, goading her further, asked if she'd like to someday own a horse, she would, because that possibility was so out of the question (she didn't make much at the store and rented half a duplex), just go quiet and blink, blink, as if something happening outside her cage had startled her into stillness.

Of course, one day she fell in love. He was a man she worked with at the store. I can see her now in the brown apron they gave her. I don't imagine he had given her any romantic signals, but they were there together every day and likely he did for her the sorts of small kindnesses people do for one another when working with one another and in time she decided he was the one for her. She started dropping his name. "That's what Randy thinks too," she'd say, or "I said that same thing to Randy the other day." We imagined that Randy thought about her the way we did; that is, in his early days of working with her, he'd waited to discover what might be special or interesting about her only to find that she didn't have, as the expression goes, much to recommend her.

She always seemed to be reading directly from a book on how to be most common.

"Are those apples fresh?" someone would ask, and she'd say, "I suppose they are pretty fresh." "Was that an earthquake just now?" someone would ask, and she'd say, "If it was, it will be on the radio."

Then came a change. Because she was in love, or fancied herself to be, with Randy, and because, I expect, she could feel that not only did he not feel the same way, he didn't feel much about her at all (and why would he, given that she was, as mentioned, experienced by most people as a slightly puzzling blankness), she started, perhaps, to panic a little, to sense, maybe for the first time in her life, that her natural way of being was not interesting enough to get the attention of (much less delight or captivate) someone like, even, Randy, who, I should say, was no font of originality himself but at least had a big truck he loved and would wash with pleasure every Friday after his shift and sometimes would at least make a dirty joke or pick up a strange-looking damaged orange and do the funny voice in which he imagined such an orange might speak, and was, for example, a passionate advocate for, and defender of, his mother, a mean old thing who lived a few houses down from the store, a strongly self-certain lightning bolt of constant opining who presented as a fierce pair of black men's glasses moving around on a tanned, agitated face.

But Randy, as they say, thought his mother hung the moon, and this was because she thought he hung it. It was a kind of mutual admiration society. He got along nicely with her. And she got along nicely with him. Which was, I thought, we all thought, part of the reason he'd never married, perhaps.

It was a small town, and we did a good deal of talking about such things.

The woman, who we called Sparrow among ourselves but whose real name, funnily enough, was Gloria, noticed this about Randy, the way he was with his mother, and added it to the growing list of things she liked about him. That is, she would say he was a good man; that you can tell a lot about a man by how he treats his mother; that mothers were God's special gift to us all. And so forth. Just all the things you would expect her to say, all the first-order things someone might say had she made no attempt to think anew about the thing in question.

Noticing that she was having no effect on Randy, she started trying new things, such as having opinions of her own. But it was as if she were just manufacturing these in

188

order to have them. "Oh, I know what!" she'd say. "We should put the fudge up there, with the olives." Or "So-and-so is such a good actor. I think I have a little crush on him." And it was always whatever actor was on the cover of some magazine that month, and if you pressed her on it you'd find she'd never seen any of his movies.

You would never have described her as feminine. But now she decided that the way to Randy's heart was to become more girlish. Somewhere she got hold of a curling iron and some perfume. Imagine that trip to the mall in Werthley. Or the one in Clover. She didn't drive. So would have taken the bus. Soon the store smelled of her new perfume. She started, based on an article in one of the women's magazines she'd begun reading, to laugh more. She would laugh at anything Randy said, and not just the things that he meant to be funny. He would look over, startled, at such a time.

We could all see a fall was coming. Randy's mother owned the store and would come in behind those big glasses, judging everything. Who the hell put the fudge way up there? she would demand. What was that terrible smell? "I'm wearing perfume,"

Gloria would say. "Well, why?" the mother would snap. "Are you going on a date?" That was the punch line: the idea of Gloria on a date with some unlucky bastard. The mother would laugh her low alcoholic growl of a laugh as if this was the most far-fetched idea ever. But she wasn't only mean. She had an honest, caring side to her, too. "Don't get your hopes up, sister, men-wise," she'd tell Gloria, in the lettuce-smelling corner of the stockroom where they piled the cardboard boxes. "You're not much to look at but . . ." And she'd think to add something like "you've got a good heart" or "you're a hard worker," but because she prided herself on being laceratingly honest, as these thoughts came up, she felt she had to not say them, because this Gloria had never shown any evidence of having an especially good heart, and as far as being a hard worker, well, no. She showed up every day, sure, but had never, in the mother's memory, taken any special interest in the workings of the store or had a single fresh, helpful idea about anything at all. It was strange to have had someone working for you for nearly two years and not be able to recall a single occasion on which she had suggested anything to improve or liven up the store, such as, that gal they'd fired,

Irene, had at least had the idea of putting a glass jar on the counter into which people could drop spare change, which would then be given to the local children's hospital, but which, it turned out, Irene was cleverly pocketing about half of. Which was why she'd been let go. So, not that clever. Although pretty clever. Because it had taken them nearly a year to catch her. But at least that Irene had shown some gumption, some desire to, well, improve her condition, one might say. She wasn't some inert thing letting life just happen to her.

Because this opinionated and sometimes caring old lady was a sharp observer, she picked up on the fact that her son was in Gloria's sights. And told him so. He just laughed. But then started to think. Not about Gloria, exactly, but about the fact of her liking him. He liked the idea of her starting to work there two years ago in a neutral state and then noticing this man who worked there, that is, him, Randy, and coming gradually to prefer him over all of the men in town and over all the men in the world, apparently, coming to like him the most, in some special way he didn't really know about yet but would like to know more about. What was it about him that she liked so much? It was interesting. He liked, also, the way they seemed to agree on everything. That wasn't the case with other women. Other women often disagreed with him. If he said it was about to rain, they might say, "I doubt it" or "Doesn't look like it" or "That's not in the forecast." But she, Gloria, would say something like "I bet you're right." Which confirmed they were simpatico. And when it did start to rain, she'd say, "It's raining cats and dogs," which seemed, to him, like a forthright way of acknowledging how right he'd been. And then (he found this generous) she'd smile, as if it pleased her to be able to acknowledge how right he'd been. Which he liked. He liked the way she noticed and enjoyed the way he tended to get most things right. She seemed, in this way, confident. It didn't bother her, the way it did most women, when he was shown to be right. If a person was right, he was right, she seemed to feel, it was no skin off her ass.

So, imagine you are a woman who, all your life, people have shied away from and avoided, and whenever you said something it went out into the world and just hung there, causing a neutral or slightly adverse reaction, and every time this happened, you felt it, and so, behind you, in your life there had accrued a series of light but painful little blows, conspiring to convince you that there was something wrong with you, and now you find yourself in the daily presence of a man who seems to be coming to like you and has even started to leave you little presents on the break room table (a chocolate mint, a single Twinkie). And imagine that this man's mother is against it, against this thing that is the thing that, now, propels you, Gloria, out of bed every morning. And that she, the mother, finds all of this amazing and laughable and disappointing and even, one day, tells her son that his interest in you is causing her to downgrade her opinion of him. And imagine that the man shares this with you. But, far from discouraging him, he says, this has actually made him feel, for the first time, that he is the protector of some woman not his mother. Which, he says, blushing, has made him feel tender, toward you, or whatnot.

Imagine the kind of month that would be for you if you were that woman.

And imagine you are that man, who, for the first time, feels he is protecting a woman not his mother, a woman who is so much more full of life than his old, tan, bent-but-agile mother, whose smug eternal certainty is, for the first time, coming to seem tiresome, as are those big honker glasses that once belonged to his father, into which she, for some reason, put new lenses last year, that is, eleven whole years after your father's passing. That woman, that young, energetic woman with whom you often now find yourself in pleasant agreement, might suddenly start to seem even prettier to you, even if no one else seems to notice it. But you notice it, this uptick in her prettiness, and say so, in one of those notes you've begun leaving on the break table, with those snacks, notes that are getting longer and longer lately and sometimes even border on the passionate, in which your grammar will sometimes go a bit off as you struggle to express these new feelings, and that might even include a drawing of, for example, a cartoon man with stars pouring out of the open top of his head.

And one day there comes a kiss. In the stockroom. After it, you say, "Not bad," to which she replies, "Not bad at all," which you take as confirmation that you are, as you have always felt yourself to be, an excellent kisser, and now someone has finally noticed it, thank you very much.

And then the two of you are off to the races, and no matter what we, the people who live in that town and shop in that store, think about it, or how we snicker about it in the parking lot, saying unimaginative things ourselves now, such as "Well, good for them, really, why not?" or "One thing I would not want to be is a fly on the wall of wherever it is they go to be alone" or "I guess you never can tell, with people," and no matter what the mother with the men's glasses might hiss at night at her son in the house, her house, that she and the son share but that she owns, there would still be, as if willed by some force bigger than any of us, a wedding, in July, in the church just up the block that had formerly been a private home and that the current pastor had crowned with a bell tower of sorts but without any bell in it.

And all of us would go to that wedding, because how could we not? And because the new couple looked so naïve, happy, and clueless, standing there at the altar of the church with no bell in its tower, we would think: "Oh, this is not going to end well."

And it may not. It still may not end well. Life being, as they say, long. But it has not ended badly yet. It has not ended at all. When we are in that store, we will often hear him singing her praises, whether she is nearby or not, and same with her: she is always singing his praises, whether he is nearby or not. Seeing her now, one does not think "looks like bird" but "small, glowing lady." And he, he moves around the store with a theatrical beneficence, seeming to take a fastidious pleasure in helping customers with even the smallest things, sometimes even helping a customer too much, for too long, not at all ashamed now, it seems, to be seen working in his mother's store, as he had so often seemed to be formerly. And over time, the mother has become, one might say, subservient to, even adoring of, the couple they have become, and, whether they are nearby or not, but especially if they are not, will sing their praises, saying that they are devoted, abso- lutely devoted to each other, is the way she will most often put it.

GHOUL

At noon Layla wheels over Vat of Lunch. For a sec I can be not-scary, leaning against our plastiform wall meant to resemble human entrails.

"Why aren't the old served first?" crabs Leonard, Squatting Ghoul Two, senior to all.

Last week Leonard's knee went out. We, his fellow Squatting Ghouls, have since been allowing him to sit upon our plastiform Remorseful Demon, which, at this moment, emits one of its periodic Remorse-groans.

"Grieve on, foul beast," I say, per Script.

"Foul indeed!" says Artie, Feuding Ghoul Four: great guy, always blurting out such quips as "Brian, you are really on it, in terms of the way you keep casting your eyes fitfully back and forth while squatting!" To which I might reply, "Thanks, Artie, you Feuding Ghouls are also ripping it up, I so admire how, every day, you guys come up with a whole new topic for your Feud!"

Into my paper bowl goes: Lunch. A broth with, plopped down in it, a single gleaming Kit Kat.

Someday I, too, may be old, knees giving out, some group of Squatting Ghouls as yet unborn (or currently mere Li'l Demons, running around in their bright red diapers) allowing elder me, kaput like Leonard, to sit on, perhaps, this very same plastiform Remorseful Demon, in that dismal future time!

Today, however, all is well: Break Week is nigh.

Next A.M., via Tram, the Break-eligible among us are taken all jolly to the Room: a cavernous space shaped exactly the same as our workhouse, MAWS OF HELL, as well as the eleven other plenteous underground workhouses within our Region. But free of the supplementary Décor that makes each workhouse a unique immersive experience. Free, as well, of Byway Paths, and the small cars on tracks that bear our delighted Visitors through us. The Room is, truth be told, just a great space for a relaxed chill-out! It has Bowling, should you choose; pretend meadow, with real-appearing flowers; free-flowing creek, beside which we may sit, out of which fake fish leap on these sort of wheels, four fish per wheel, smiling, as if to say, "Leaping is what we love!"

Plus we each get a niche into which to put our stuff.

In the Room, we may mingle with individuals from our sister workhouses, such as BENEATH OUR MOTHER THE SEA or WILD DAY OUT WEST. May we mate there? Sure. We may. Many do. Should you observe someone mating and wish to be polite? Lurch off suddenly, as if you have left something back in your niche. Sometimes (tight quarters in the Room!) you may need to step or hop over a mating pair. The polite thing: step or hop over, saying nada. Should you personally know one or both, and feel saying nada might violate politeness, well, say something encouraging, such as "Go, go, go!" or "Looking good, James and Melissa, all best wishes!"

Today, hopping over two such folks, I think, Hey, isn't that Mr. Tom Frame, normally the "Before" manifestation of Monk Decapitated for Evil Thoughts, in the portion of MAWS OF HELL called "Payback's a Mother"? Mr. Frame, out of his seventeenth-century-monk threads, is mating with Gwen Thorsen, one of our rotating team of folks in hooded robes playing

199

Death, and here I did not even know that Mr. Frame even knew her!

"Hey, Tom, hi, Gwen!" I cry, not wishing to violate politeness.

To which both briefly glance up at me all love-faced.

That is another great thing about Break Week: you are always seeing folks in new contexts!

For example, last Break, I saw Rolph Spengler, Flying Spear Launcher Three, quietly drinking tea, writing in his journal. No wings on, face not painted red, no wire elevating him aloft, no cloven-hoofed boots. Actually, he looked so tender in the face I felt the need of asking what he was writing.

"A letter to my son," he said.

"I did not even know you had a son, Rolph!" I said.

"Well," he said.

"I guess so, if you are writing to your son!" I said. "All I ever saw you as? A red-painted, big-winged, cloven-hoofed fellow, flinging down your spears."

"And I guess all I ever saw you as was a tiny Squatting Ghoul, far below me," Rolph said. "Whom I kept trying to just barely miss with my spears. My son is Edgar, CHICAGO GANGSTER HIDEOUT."

And, just like that, we became friends!

Now whenever Rolph, on wire, hovers over our quadrant, he will wave down at me with his non-spear hand, at which I will rise from my squat and throw my arms wide, exposing my chest, as if to say, "Spear me, then, Flying Spear Launcher! Since I am already a Squatting Ghoul, how much worse can my afterlife even get?" At which Rolph will fake-pump his spear at me, as if to say, "Ha ha, talk to you next Break, pal!"

By which I mean: friendship may take time and faith to grow!

(Please note: whenever Rolph and I engage in our fun ritual, no Visitors are present. As if! As if Rolph and I would risk providing our Visitors a subpar experience in that way. No, we engage in this warm friendship exchange only when no Visitors are near. Which is so rarely the case. Normally we are just swamped!)

Moments after hopping over Gwen and Mr. Frame, I find Mr. Frame sitting across from me at Lunch, in Dining, explaining why he, a married man, was just now mating with Gwen.

Mr. Frame's wife, Ann Frame, used to be on Guillotine-Cart Pull Team Five. Those guillotines, being heavy, needing to be pulled over some fake rough terrain, which, though made of poly, still must be bumpy to seem real, Ann's back went out, and she was transferred to VICTORIAN WEEKEND, a big adjustment, since, instead of being scary, she had to adopt a mindset of mincing and serving. Now she is Cockney Cook: sweet gig! All she has to do is, every half hour, blunder into this formal dining hall, interrupting some Royals (Visitors) eating in there, then blunder out, knocking over a tea cart while apologizing for her humble class origins in a Cockney accent. But alas: apparently, her new role has caused marital stress, because Mrs. Frame is now constantly practicing her Cockney accent, even while on Break, in the Room.

I try to be a pal by pointing out that Tom himself always takes ample care, prior to the moment of his decapitation, to appear genuinely terrified. Also, re the lightning-burst-thunderclap spate of total darkness that allows him to switch the headless "After" Animatron in for himself on the chopping block before he hops down the DisaHole: does he not always endeavor to do that quickly, so the switch will go unnoticed by our Visitors? Maybe, I suggest, he is more like Ann than he wishes to acknowledge! Isn't his quick hopping analogous to Ann's continually practicing her ac-

cent, i.e., a form of admirable professional-
ism?

"I guess what I'm saying is, I don't practice hopping into the DisaHole when we're
on Break," he says.

"I get that," I say, listening and agreeing
being a proven path to friendship. "That
sounds frustrating."

"But she just goes on and on," he says.
" 'Guv'n'r' this, 'guv'n'r' that. And why?
For what?"

"Wants to do a good job?" I say. "For her
Visitors?"

"Of whom there never are any?" he says,
crossly.

Then there is this rather big silence.

"Not that I'm saying there never are any,"
he says.

"I know you're not saying that, Tom," I
say.

"I should probably just shut up," he says.

"Probably," I say.

Jeez, I think, Tom, Mr. Frame, you have
really put me in a bad spot!

Rules are rules, friends are friends. But
now rules and friends urge differing courses
of action upon me, and which shall I
choose?

I take a long thinking-walk along our fake

creek, pondering, and see several false ducks there, belly up, being serviced by Todd Sharpe. When Todd gets something right, a quack can be heard, or at least part of one.

Gosh! I am usually all about Team. When my back went out last year, did I discontinue squatting and stand up straight, which would have felt good? No, I squatted on, using a broken-off broom as a brace. Once, filling in as Screaming Doomed Cleric, though I had strep, I screamed for eight straight hours, even providing all six Optional Dread Whoops.

Yet I continue pacing the free-flowing creek, going back and forth from one wall where the creek ends in a painting of itself flowing off into eternity to the other, until finally Todd has every last duck up and running, except for one too broke to ever quack again, which Todd bears away under one of his arms.

Just then, from near Bowling, I hear both hue and cry.

And rush over to find a group informally gathered around my pal Rolph Spengler, Flying Spear Launcher Three, engaging in some kicking activity, as Rolph continues, despite the kicking, to emit such discredited ideas as: "We pass our days enacting insane rituals of denial with which I, for one, am

done! Can't we just admit and discuss?"
And: "Truth, truth! Can't we just, for once,
speak the goddamn —"

Jeez! No wonder that group around Rolph
is kicking him!

Shirley from Monitoring shoots me a look,
meaning: Brian, give Rolph there a kick, so
I can write down that you were among those
who gave Rolph a kick because you were, as
we all were, shocked and offended by the
boldness and audacity of Rolph's lies and,
wishing to do your part in sparing the larger
community the burden of Rolph's confu-
sion, you, with your foot or feet, did your
best to stem the tide of twisted negativity
pouring forth from strange, discredited
Rolph.

At this point, in fairness, Rolph is no
longer saying his lies. He is just inert.
Shirley's eyes go wide, then glance down at
my foot, as if to say, "Brian, I know you are
one of the good guys and I would like to be
able to write that down."

It is not a true kick I give Rolph, more of
a foot-tap.

But it is that foot-tap, as I stumble away,
that gives me pause. Leaning against a fake
elm still in its ancient shipping box, I think,
That tap did not hurt Rolph, probably. Not
much. Then, with my right foot, I foot-tap

my left calf, in order to feel what Rolph felt. Then again, harder. It should be a comfort to me: even when I foot-tap my own calf a ton harder than I actually foot-tapped Rolph, it doesn't hurt that much at all.

Still, it might have felt unpleasant if one was dying as one felt it.

Wait, where was I going again? I ask my-self.

Monitoring & Reporting Services, I reply. To rat out Tom.

Thanks, I respond.

If you don't wish to be dealt with harshly, don't do anything wrong, I underscore.

Just be normal, I concur.

At least it is quick to cross the Main Plain, because, on this unsettling day, absolutely no one is mating.

Across Bridge C looms Monitoring & Reporting Services: trim mauve hut, many fluttering banners.

As I approach the bridge, my name is called, and I turn to find Gabrielle D. of FIFTIES SOCK HOP, chomping gum as usual, in bobby socks though sixty, along with her husband, Bill, whose letter sweater, it seems, grows tighter by the day. And who is always calling me Frankenstein. What is up with that? Inaccurate! Do I call him Eisenhower just because that individual is of Bill's same theme-milieu?

Though on Break, hence not required to be in costume, they are. Plus Bill is wearing his hair slicked back and Gabrielle D. has retained her normal flouncy ponytail.

"What's the haps, Frankie?" Bill says. "Frankenstein? Frank-a-roo?"

"Hi, Bill," I say.

"Tom Frame asked us to slap this bit of scribble on you, babycakes," Gabrielle D. says.

And hands me a note, which I read on the spot:

Dear Brian,
Please know that I have taken my recent error to heart and am thinking deeply upon it in order to decrease the likelihood of making a similar mistake in the future. When I said that thing about no Visitors ever coming down here, please know that I did not mean it and was, in my awkward way, making an attempt at facetiousness. Or, I said it in fun, being ironical, to indicate how fiercely I believe in its very opposite.
Because I consider myself a person of conscience, I feel compelled to underscore that once your Reporting Period is over,

you too will have committed a crime, one of omission. Please know that should you opt to Report me, I will understand. However, if you opt not to Report me, I will consider us bonded forever into the future by the great kindness you will have shown me.

With thanks, in eternal friendship, no matter what you decide,

Please destroy this message,

Tom Frame

"Any response, monster-man?" Bill says.

"Not at this time, Bill," I say.

"We're hip to that, daddy-o," Gabrielle D. says, and off they go, holding hands, and then, as is often the case, they pause so he can dip her.

Now I must just cross the bridge and rat Tom out.

But what a nice letter, how direct and trusting.

I turn on my heel, hit Vending up for a potpie, take it home, eat it in my Sleep Slot, go nowhere all night.

And, in this way, allow my Reporting Period to expire.

Yet how ironic.

Next morning, post-Breakfast, I am squatting near my niche, having a Gingerade, when up trots, all peppy, Amy, Special Assistant to Shirley of Monitoring.

"Hey, Bri," she says. "Got a sec? Some of us were going through your niche just now? And look what I found."

In her hand: that letter Mr. Frame wrote me that was so nice!

In her other hand: her whistle, which, I feel, at any second, she may blow on me.

"Just so you know?" she says. "Moments ago, I showed Mr. Frame this letter. After which, he very openly ratted you out, claiming that, yesterday, he blurted out a Regrettable Falsehood in your presence, and that you, at that time, gave him a look indicating that you wouldn't turn him in. Which, per my records, you haven't. Turned him in. Brian, I need some honesty here: did Mr. Frame, yesterday, blurt out a Regrettable Falsehood?"

"Yes," I say.

"But you didn't turn him in," she says.

"I guess not?" I say. "Not yet?"

"Are you turning him in now?" she says.

"Did he really turn me in?" I say.

"I just detailed that to you," she says. "Yes."

"Then yes," I say.

"And yet your Reporting Period is expired," she says.

"Is it?" I say.

"And Mr. Frame is claiming immunity, for being First Individual Forthcoming," she says.

Three cowboys from WEST amble by, fake-bowlegged.

And tip their huge hats at us.

"Brian, to be frank?" she says. "We were kids together. Remember TinyGhosts, remember BabyDracs, remember we were on the Teen Crew that built those first, hilariously inept Torture Racks? I really don't want to blow this whistle and have a group gather and kick you to death."

"I'd also prefer that not to happen," I say.

"But you see my dilemma, though, right?" she says. "Mr. Frame just ratted you out, for not ratting him out. Who's to say he might not rat me out if I fail to blow my whistle on you? See what I mean? Bri, are you willing to work with me on this?"

"Very much so," I say.

"Stay quiet and nod," she says. "During what follows."

And blows her whistle.

A crowd gathers.

Amy, trusted by all, gives a disillusioned shake of her sad, dispirited head.

"Moments ago," she says, "a Regrettable

Falsehood was uttered aloud."

A gasp goes up, and across dozens of faces there runs a ripple of: You've got to be kidding, this outrage makes us suddenly so mad.

"By Tom Frame," Amy says.

She looks at me.

I nod.

"We know this," Amy says, "because Brian here, doing his duty, though it was difficult, spoke the truth. To me. Just now. Immediately. Don't be surprised if Mr. Frame, a self-admitted liar, now tries making some further shit up to save his butt."

The crowd rushes off to find Mr. Frame.

"I just couldn't blow my whistle on you," Amy says. "I've found you cute since we were little."

"I've found you cute, too," I say.

Which I haven't, that much, but it seems like a bad moment to begin violating politeness.

Soon, from the sounds Mr. Frame makes when the crowd finds him over by Vending, it becomes clear that the crowd has found Mr. Frame over by Vending.

Amy and I stand there listening, making silent winces of *eek* and *ouch.*

"I guess one never realizes how little one wants to be kicked to death until one hears a crowd doing that exact same thing to someone nearby," I say.

"The thing is," Amy says, "Mr. Frame actually did that for which he is right now being punished. So I don't need to feel bad about that. Do I?"

"No," I say.

"What I need to feel bad about, I suppose, is that you also did something bad, for which you have not yet been punished," she says. "Jeez. And now I'm doing something bad, for which I may later be punished. You make me not even care about right or wrong, though."

Then we kiss. And, finding a place beside the free-flowing creek, mate. It is not my first time, but I have to say it is one of my best, my relief that I am not being kicked to death by a group of my peers being, I think, what makes it so memorable.

On my way back to my niche, I pass Mr. Frame. There he is, fallen, by Vending. One of our sickly little birds lands on Mr. Frame and gives him a peck. How do those birds get down here, anyway? That is one of our abiding mysteries. What would impel them to fly down our Egress Spout? Or have they been down here always?

Oh, Tom, I think, it's my fault, I should have thrown your letter away. But I treasured it and hoped to read it many more times. But mostly, Tom, it's your fault, for ratting me out to Amy, after she busted you for doing the wrong thing that you truly did do, after which you tried to claim the immunity that stems from being First Individual Forthcoming. What was up with that, Tom? Had you succeeded in ratting me out, it would be me, not you, being pecked by a sickly bird near Vending, looking much the worse for wear, Tom.

To which Tom, long gone, emits a hissing sound from the zone near his mouth.

That night Amy comes over and sleeps with me in my Sleep Slot: tight fit! Wedged in there so tight that neither of us can roll over unless we both do so at the same time, we mate, we laugh, we slide ourselves out and cook noodles on my hot plate, then slide ourselves back in and she teaches me how to braid her hair.

Although for many years I did not think of Amy as all that cute, I do now.

In the morning, I wake to find her forehead touching mine. On her face is a look that says, Can I just say something?

"Good morning," I say.

"I'm not sure I can do this," she says.

"It is pretty tight in here," I say.

"All my life I've tried to do everything right," she says. "And now this. Here I am, a Special Assistant, and what am I doing? Exactly the opposite."

She is slated to Monitor DISCO LOVE NEST and now begins crankily costuming up from a daypack she brought along last night.

"Seeing Tom dead wigged me out, I admit it," she says. "Because, in a sense, we caused that. I mean, we did. We got Tom Frame kicked to death and now he rests in peace or wherever. For me? It came down to: Okay, so who do I want to see kicked to death less, Brian or Tom? And the answer was you. So I lied. And I guess now I'm just going to have to live with that."

"You saved my life," I say.

"God, I know, but still, ugh," she says.

When I pull the pulley that causes the bed to slide out, guess what?

A one-time incident involving excess water presence has occurred.

Is occurring.

All kinds of junk is floating past: a cape, a fake arm, a lunch box.

Amy, nice short disco boot perched above the ongoing water incident, purses her lips, as in: I love these boots, this is so not fair.

But step down she does. She must. Or be late. The water runs into her boots, as I take

214

her hand, all VICTORIAN WEEKEND.

"Shit," she says. "I hate this."

A silence hangs above us, as in: Hate what, Amy?

Red Murray comes sloshing past, chasing the Swiss hat he must wear for his ALPS RESORT role, Mountaineer Famous for Surviving Terrible Avalanche.

No way is Red catching that hat.

Going past, he shoots me this look of: This should be easy but somehow that darn thing keeps eluding my grasp.

"These seem to be getting worse," I say.

"What do?" Amy says.

"Nothing," I say.

We slosh along, holding hands, and I am overcome by a powerful feeling of trusting and liking and wishing to be brought even closer to this person whose eyelashes last night flickered against mine in the night, with mine also flickering against hers, a pretty bonding thing to do with someone, especially while mating with them.

So I just say it.

"These floods," I say softly.

And find her stopped, looking down shocked at the water flowing into and around her short disco boots.

I have put her in a bad spot. And me in a bad spot.

215

Have put the two of us in a bad spot.

She leans in close.

"Flood," she whispers.

"Flood," I whisper back.

"Stupid flood," she whispers, a bit giddily.

Then the lights flicker and all goes dark.

"Power failure," Amy whispers.

"*Another* power failure," I whisper back right away, so she will not doubt for even a second that I am all the way with her.

"Visitors are coming," she whispers sarcastically in the dark.

"So many Visitors," I say.

The lights come back on and quickly gaining on us is Gwen Thorsen, dressed as Death, heading to the Tram, holding her Death robe up out of what, we realize, we have just called, out loud, possibly within her earshot, "flood," after which we both uttered aloud the problematic phrase "power failure," referring to that which it would have been best to bear silently with good grace, after which we both uttered aloud the most Regrettable Falsehood one can utter.

Gwen's eyes narrow into these slits of: (1) Yes, guys, I heard all that just now, and (2) You two are having a thing, which is great, but, think about it, you killed Tom Frame, with whom I myself was having a thing.

In her haste to go rat us out, she drops the train of her Death robe and it trails behind her, making a temporary road of wave in the water.

"Crap," Amy says.

And blows her whistle.

A crowd gathers, many rubbing their eyes, having only just now awoken.

"Gwen here just uttered a Regrettable Falsehood aloud," Amy says. "Concerning what, I'd rather not say, but . . ."

Then twirls the toe of her disco boot in the water.

"I didn't!" Gwen says. "She did! And he did. They also, both, used the problematic phrase 'power failure,' as well as —"

"Which, hello, you yourself just used," Amy says.

"I used it to point out that you used it!" Gwen says. "Earlier."

"I find this tragic," Amy says. "Gwen, you are just playing a very weak game of turn-around."

In Gwen's eyes, I can see that she knows she can't win against Amy, so well trusted by all.

"Wait," Gwen says, frantic. "Think about it, guys. Isn't it possible that Amy is the one — is the lying one? And not me? If they, in fact, said those things that I just now claimed they said, and I overheard them, wouldn't this be, uh, exactly how she would, you know, approach it?"

Even though I know Gwen is telling the truth, she is telling it so nervous even I doubt it.

During the kicking that ensues, Amy gives me a look with furrowed brow, as in: Get in there, man.

I get in there. I don't kick or even foot-tap, just stand there in the early-morning-breath smell of it all, being jostled by my peers' abundant kicking.

Oh, Gwen, I think, why did you not do what I have so often done upon overhearing someone saying something I wished I wasn't overhearing, namely, pretend I wasn't hearing it?

When all is done, someone suggests that, out of respect, we heft Gwen, always a sweetheart until now, off the wet floor and set her on something higher, such as the Suggestion Box, made of plastic, shaped like a giant rose, in which we may leave Suggestions, should we so choose.

We drape Gwen over the rose, which, sensing her there, goes, "Great idea! I love it!"

Because Gwen continues to be draped

218

across it, the rose keeps saying that as we drift away.

"This is going from bad to worse," Amy says as we approach the Tram.

"I'll say," I say.

"I suppose you think I went to the whistle too quick," she says. "Oh, God, maybe I did. But what did you want me to do? Let her go rat us out, so we could spend the rest of the day waiting to get kicked to death? Does that sound fun? Why were we talking all that crap anyway? What were we thinking?"

Looking over at her there, in her disco boots, eyes moist with tears, appearing not hot but a bit odd and out of sorts, I find myself feeling more tenderly toward her than I would were she looking all composed and hot — i.e., her moment of weakness and being flustered is calling forth feelings of wishing to protect her from all future harm.

At the Tram, upset, she will not kiss me.

But I insist. And we do. Kiss. And continue kissing, even as she, on the Tram, must therefore slightly bend, and I must slightly jog, for us to continue kissing.

Then the Tram disappears into Tunnel Eight.

I turn to regard the Room and find it

shimmering, its fake trees AutoSwaying in sync, the tinkle and glow of the many tiny lights upon the trees reflected in the delicate leaping-fish-caused ripples of the free-flowing creek, all of this saying to me, Brian, you feel bad about what just now happened to Gwen, sure, okay, fair enough, but, for all that, is it not still a beautiful world? Which you would not even be in anymore, if not for Amy, who, at this point, has saved your life twice?

Why not try being happy?

That afternoon, those of us on Break gather as a community beneath the Egress Spout.

Before us: three silver body bags, labeled "R.S.," "T.F.," and "G.T.," respectively.

Entering with her fellow Monitors, Amy casts a glance at me, her long shiny hair relocating, then swinging back to where it was pre-swing, her winsome glance seeming to say, Ah, sweet, you again!

Then her look grows somber, as in: Ugh, I just remembered, two of those three silver bags lying there all lumpy are due in part to us.

Mr. Regis from Workhouse Effective Co-ordination says a few words through his little amp, re how sad it is to live out one's whole life honoring certain timeless principles, then throw that all away in one ill-advised moment, and in the name of what? Disorder? Chaos? Thus taking one's dishonor forward into all eternity.

The lights flicker, go off, come back on.

Have we found this life pleasant? Mr. Regis asks. Have we found people to be fond of, things that give us pleasure? Have we generally felt, getting up in the morning, that, if we lived within Law 6, our days would go well? Is it too much to ask that certain false, negative things not be underscored? Is it totally crazy that those who, for their own selfish reasons, insist on underscoring certain false, negative things shall be rebuked?

Al from Janitorial steps forward, picks up the "R.S." bag, disappears briskly up the Egress Spout.

Dennis from Janitorial steps forward, picks up the "T.F." bag, disappears up the Egress Spout, albeit less briskly, since Dennis is smaller than Al and Tom was bigger than Rolph.

Soon, Rolph and Tom will rest Above, in that shady graveyard near Pueblo (Colorado) depicted on the Memorial Prayer Cards now being handed out by Susan and Gabe of Consolation Services, Pueblo (Colorado) being the city under which we

221

are approximately located.

Gwen must yet abide here a bit longer, until Al and Dennis come down and decide which one of them will lug her up Above.

Mr. Regis unplugs the mic from his little amp, picks up the little amp, walks sadly off, if one can be said to walk sadly while carrying a little amp.

Amy, departing, sneaks me a wave.

Oh, Life, I think, I wish you were simpler and I could have these growing feelings of love for Amy without the countervailing negative feelings that stem from, in a sense, our having played a part in certain recent undesirable occurrences.

And find myself somewhat cursing Law 6 in my heart.

To which Life says: Why curse Law 6 about it? Had you stayed within its sensible guidance and ratted out Tom immediately, and refrained from talking a bunch of Regrettable crap aloud with Amy right in front of Gwen, then Tom would be just as dead as he is now, as is appropriate, and Gwen would still be alive, romping around in her Death robe with that goofy crooked smile on her face as usual, and you could just be enjoying your feelings for Amy, no problem, the two of you working hard, anticipating Visitors, thinking, perhaps, of marriage, maybe, eventually, of babies, like normal people, law-abiding folks.

All of which sounds good.

But, alas, is not to be.

Guy comes up, holding a tommy gun.

"Are you by any chance Brian?" he says. "Dad mentioned you. He really got a kick out of fake-menacing you from above, I guess? I had a feeling it was you. Because Dad sent me a sketch. Dad was such a talented artist. I'm Edgar Spengler, CHICAGO GANGSTER HIDEOUT. Rolph's son! Sorry about the gun. I came right over from Role."

The sketch shows me as I am when Squatting Ghoul Eight: Hell-scorched shirt, fire-blackened slacks, smoldering necktie, meant to communicate that, pre-Death, I was an office worker, perhaps even Exec.

Under it, Rolph has written in calligraphy: "Edgar, this is Brian, that friend I have made."

I tell Edgar that Rolph was a good man.

"Well, Mom and I always thought so," Edgar says. "We truly have no clue what got into him there at the end. He was always so sane. Just happy, you know? Anyway, right before his unfortunate, but deserved, passing, Dad, done with Break, about to head back to MAWS, asked me to get this sketch to you. Then I forgot. Oops. Kind of ironic. Oh, and this."

Then hands me a letter. Which I step aside to read:

Dear Brian,

I sense in you a "kindred spirit." So am about to lay some heavy truth on you.

A certain dark knowledge has been eating away at me for some thirty years now. I am old and hereby pass this troubling wisdom-flame from my cupped palm to yours. Have I told my son, Edgar, of CHICAGO GANGSTER HIDEOUT? No. Edgar, God love him, has always been a super straight arrow, lacking imagination, although a better heart you will never encounter, and I have always feared this would be too much for him and that, being as literal as he is, he might indeed rat me out, his own father.

Long ago, I was a teenager. With a ton of ornery energy. Which drove me, one night (brace yourself!), to enter and climb up the Egress Spout. True story! I had balls like a bull. In those days. Up I went, up that chrome ladder with which all are familiar, which, as you know, it is verboten to touch, much less climb, thinking, in my hubris: I'll just see what Above is like, witnessing for myself some of what we were taught in Geography, e.g., candy stores, viaducts, rain, boulevards, football "tailgate" parties, hiking up mountains, tanning poolside, kissing one's girl in something called "parking area behind Safeway." I would so love to see Sky, I thought. So high and all. And those forests must be just super green this time of season.

Climbed for forty to fifty minutes. Then, whammo, found my neck suddenly bent.

By what?

Low ceiling of rock.

That is correct: the Egress Spout goes up, yes, but as far as Egress? There is none (!). The Spout is merely a long vertical tunnel terminating in that ceiling of rock against which, as mentioned, climbing fast, I bent my neck.

What about the bodies of our beloved dead, you may ask, which, year after year, we have watched being lugged up the Spout, to Above, by Dennis and Al, and, prior to that, by Bob "Big Bob" French?

Yes, right, exactly!

Starting down, I discovered, off to one side, a cavelike room that, in my haste and the dark, I had missed on the way up, and if you're the type to get creeped out by a

225

big pile of silver body bags, some dating back fifty, sixty years, with a faint smell of decay, and the random skeletal arm or leg jutting out, take my advice: don't go in there with a flashlight, as I erroneously did!

In summary, the Spout up which we all have been hopefully gazing these many years is no Spout at all, but a mere shaft leading to a sad, creepy room of the dead(!).

We are sealed in, sealed in good down here, by a stout, permanent plug of concrete. Or perhaps a concrete/poly amalgam.

How are Visitors supposed to get down here? They aren't. They were not, it seems, ever intended to.

We shall remain un-Visited forever.

I shit you not.

What's it about? Why put us here? Once upon a time, bad things going on Above? Disease stuff, war stuff, famine stuff? Somebody Above thought: Better set a little something aside? Like seeds? And that is us? Until such time as the bad stuff ends? Or population control? Our ancestors were crooks, and this was their jail? Then why make it so fancy? Why the costumes, the roles, the creek, the Tram, the Bowling?

226

I do not know.

And believe no one currently alive among us does.

My entire adult life I have kept this to myself. I have been so lonely. Am about to blow. There are days I honestly feel like cutting my own wire with one of my spears and plummeting down from on high. But if that does not occur, see you soon, pal, from on high! I await your reply. Write me back asap, by way of Edgar, my son, CHICAGO GANGSTER HIDEOUT, who brought you this letter, although he is ignorant of its contents, and anyway has never been a big reader.

Your friend, still, I hope, despite the heavy deal I have just laid on you.

Rolph P. Spengler

I walk over and gaze up the Egress Spout, thinking, Wait, what now?

Did I know, dear reader, that few Visitors have tended to come down here, and in fact none ever has, even once, in all the days of my life? Yes, yes, of course, we all know that. But knowing it is one thing, saying it another. Why say it? Does it help? We know from bitter experience it does not. All recall with shame that period referred to as the Slough, during which, discouraged, many of us abandoned our roles entirely, casting aside accoutrements and costumes, just lolling around talking crap, arguing, kvetching, brawling, hitting Vending up for those sedative shooters called SomnoSlams, following these, sometimes minutes later, with those mini-paks of stimulant dust called the HyperHooper.

Those were the days.

Not!

Our loss of sense of purpose resulted in eight deaths across our eleven sister workhouses and the destruction of many of the cool things bequeathed to us by previous generations. One evening, that earlier described Remorseful Demon was sent tumbling down the Cliff of Unceasing Desire, emitting a sad, random Remorse-groan with each slam until, finally, boinking a Ventilation Unit, it fell silent. And lay looking up with its sad Demonic eyes at those of us who had just rolled it down there, as if to say, "Colleagues, enough, fetch me forth from this foul ravine, let us begin anew. We must believe in something, mustn't we?"

Soon, as a community, we answered: Yes. Yes, we must. Believing in nothing, we are simply going nuts! Eight dead, forty wounded? Our three main Vending Stations split open and afloat in the Central Fire

Pool, the Tram derailed so that, when going on Break, we had to walk darkened tracks to the Room, plus, what fun was Break when one had accrued absolutely zero Role Hours?

Hence Law 6.

And things got better.

And still are.

Always, I have wondered (we have all wondered, or have tried our best to wonder): When will Visitors come? Any day now. On a certain day. Which, when it begins, will be called, by us, at that time, today. Hence, every day, as we wake to a new today, we must assume that today may be the day! And when Visitors do come, what do we hope to do? Wow them. Perhaps blow their minds. With how good we are. In our case, the case of maws, how scary. How sad it would be if, after all this waiting, when our Visitors did come, we were to stink! And they were like: It was sure hard, climbing down that long Egress Spout via that slippery chrome ladder, and now, neither scared nor wowed, we must wearily climb back up it?

But it now appears that that certain day, that longed-for today, will never come.

With a start I note I am standing at the head or foot of Gwen's silver bag.

Head.

In there somewhere is whatever is left of her goofy crooked smile.

And in a sad flash it hits me: if Visitors are never coming, Gwen, Rolph, and Tom died for naught.

Not to mention Lester "Dash" Cobb, of Food Services, who, for a hobby, maintained a database of all of our birthdays, until last Christmas Eve, when, drunk, he perpetuated the dearth-of-Visitors fallacy aloud and paid the ultimate price, and never thereafter shyly handed over a crude homemade birthday card again. Or Betty Loomis, Blood-Stirring Mistress, whose role was to stand waist-deep and keening in the Pool of Guilty Blood, who, last year, took to sitting depressed on the shore, not keening even a bit, muttering things she ought not, and who, as she was encircled, blessed and forgave us all in advance.

And others, so many others.

Sometimes in life the foundation upon which one stands will give a tilt, and everything one has previously believed and held dear will begin sliding about, and suddenly all things will seem strange and new.

This happens to me now.

In truth, I am filled with wonder.

Fresh air is constantly coming to us via

Ventilation Units 1 through 26, and fresh water via our various Spigots, and food via the narrow Food Chutes that feed into our many Kitchens, and electric power, albeit sporadically, via those big green wires up there, bolted into the ceiling. None of that crap can be cheap, right? Hence there must be someone up there who still cares about us?

But what kind of caring is that? To drop folks in a hole, plug said hole up?

Oddly, it is in this moment that I realize I am in love.

Because, asking myself with whom I might share these revelations (to whom I wish to turn, in this, my hour of need), I realize it is:

Amy. Amy and only Amy.

Who, per the clock on the side of the Spout, is likely at Dinner, in Dining.

Looking for Amy as I enter, stuck behind a group from WILD DAY OUT WEST, I feel like going, "Oh, Jimbo, stop saying 'I reckon,' " as Jimbo, whose real name is Jim but who insists on WESTifying it even while on Break, stands there chewing a stir stick as if it were a piece of hay or whatnot, to look, I guess, more WEST?

The time for roles is done, Jimbo.

No Amy.

Why can't these cowpokes step aside? I somewhat crossly muse. Then take a seat, as far away from them as I can get.

Honestly, surprisingly, I find myself filled with hope. What new life might we now begin, free of the prospect of ever being Visited? Who might we become, sans roles? Toward what more generous purpose might we direct our considerable, until-now-misspent energies?

All these questions, I feel eager to explore with Amy.

Only too bad.

The Monitors of our Monitors are Shirley and Kiko: Shirley in the day and Kiko in the night.

It is thus rare to see Shirley and Kiko together in the same place.

Yet here they are now, ambling side by side into Dining.

Headed straight for me.

"Shirley tells me that wasn't much of a kick you gave Rolph the other day," Kiko says, spinning around a chair to sit in it backward.

While Shirley stays sternly standing.

"More of a nudge," Shirley says. "With the foot."

232

What a strange set of feelings I am feeling.

"Can me and Kiko buy you a Coke?" Shirley says, and offers me ten tokens.

"Have a Coke, collect your wits," says Kiko. "You have always been, so far, fairly solid."

I take the tokens, get up, and buy, actually, two Cokes, because today is Twofer-Tuesday, wherein you get two of whatever you order for the price of just one of those things.

"We're such generally nice people, our community," Kiko says, before I am even all the way sitting down. "Do you ever wonder why, occasionally, we're so violent?"

"Maybe it's because we care," says Shirley.

"I think that's exactly right," Kiko says. "We live in close quarters, and hence, to preserve positivity and order, have developed a system distinguished by its rigor, discipline, and ferocity."

Kiko's fingering her whistle, on an orange cord there around her neck.

And now sees me looking at it.

And casts a quick glance around Dining.

"Decent-sized group in here today," she says.

"Do you have anything you'd like to tell us, Brian?" Shirley says. "Anything at all?"

"We hear you're having a thing with Amy," says Kiko.

"My Special Assistant," says Shirley.

"We find ourselves having some doubts about this whole Gwen situation," says Kiko.

"With respect to Amy," says Shirley.

"With respect to Amy's apparent shocking lack of judgment," says Kiko.

"Based on the testimony of two solid eyewitnesses," says Shirley.

"Bret Freeze, Katy Freeze," says Kiko.

"We'd like to underscore that, in terms of you, all is not lost," says Shirley. "You're in a position to be First Individual Forthcoming."

"We have bigger fish to fry," says Kiko.

"To land a giant, well-respected fish like Amy," Shirley says, "a strong body of evidence is going to be key."

Poor dears! It all seems so petty.

Knowing what I now know.

I slide to them, between my Cokes, Rolph's letter.

And watch their faces go red as they read.

"So, uh, let me get this straight, Bri," Shirley says, sliding it back. "If I'm understanding this right. All these years, Dennis and Al have just been, what? Stashing those death bags up in this, um, cave, or what have you?"

"Must be getting pretty crowded up there," Kiko says.

"So crowded that whenever Dennis and Al go up there to add someone new to the mix," Shirley says, "they basically have to heave-ho the corpse up as far as they can, onto this, what? Teetering, slippery hill of the dead?"

"Easy, Shirl," says Kiko.

"And now they're all worried that next time will be the occasion on which the deceased comes sliding down and zips over the edge and a few minutes later comes shooting out of the frigging Spout?" says Shirley. "Which, how is that *my* deal?"

Then looks at me with eyes suddenly wet. To my amazement.

"Well, shit, congrats, Bri," she says hoarsely. "You've just joined a small fraternity, sworn to secrecy for the good of all."

"Don't tell Amy," Kiko says. "Do not. The fewer folks who know the better."

"All the more reason for Amy to go," says Shirley. "For you to help us get her gone."

Just then, guess who steps in?

"Speak of the devil," says Kiko.

Seeing me there with Kiko and Shirley, whose forward-leaning, extractive postures must be familiar to her from the many times she herself has assumed that posture while

235

trying to get someone to rat out a person near and dear, Amy stops in her tracks, gives me a heartbroken head tilt, sprints out of Dining.

Kiko raises her whistle and does a double toot, meaning not "Come all, kick away" but, rather, "Tate and/or Jacqueline, bring your Stunners, Stun Brian here, who seems inclined to get up and race after Amy."

There follows the earsplitting sound of an All-Alert, and Ken DiRogini, over the P.A., says an unknown individual, female, possibly Amy, actually almost for sure Amy, has just shoved Al down and illegally entered the Egress Spout, bent, apparently, on escape to Above.

And here comes Jacqueline, with her Stunner.

Down I go.

How strange to wake in Clinic, burn marks on both temples, the taste and smell of Amy and the feel of her hand in my hand fresh in my mind, only to realize that she is not Above, not at all, but trapped in that creepy cave of the dead, mulling two options equally blah: (1) Come down, be kicked to death more energetically than usual, due to having admitted her guilt via fleeing, or (2) Stay up there among the creepy dead forever, sneaking down now and then at night to hit up Vending for food and water, which, one false move and — see (1), above.

Might I rise and join her? Make a life with her? Up there? Yes. Yes. As soon as I am not so pukey. And can stay awake somewhat.

But alas.

A third option I do not imagine: that night, here comes Amy, plummeting head-first down the Spout, hitting the floor with the sound a person makes when he or she has fallen from a height it takes forty to fifty minutes to attain by ladder.

In her clenched hand: a note, to me, on a page from her Monitoring Pad, which I am handed the next morning, on the sly, in Clinic, by Carver D., Shy Suitor, VICTORIAN WEEKEND.

"Thanks, Carve," I say.

"It is of no import to one such as I," he says.

Dear Brian,

I've been waiting for you up here but no dice. I guess that would have been too much to ask. I get why you had to rat me out. I probably would have done the same. That is just how we are.

Guess what? The Spout does not lead to Above. All that's up here? A mass grave in a cave. Tom and Rolph and Gwen are here. I could reach out and touch Gwen. There, just did. Going a little bonkers in this small space in which I find myself sitting, between her and the long drop. Checking around, have located your mom, my dad. Your dad, my mom must be further in, as they died earlier?

It has sometimes in the past occurred to me that Above might not even be real. But as I write, light of an entirely new type pours in through dozens of tiny cracks in the plug.

So, Above is real, but it is not meant for us.

Everything feels broken in my head. Do you have any idea how many times I blew my whistle? On how many people? I have been sitting here trying to come up with a number. Why was I doing all that?

Sweetie, no one is coming. To see how good we have done/are doing. It is just us. Forever. Until a flood gets us or the air or food stops coming. What a joke, the way we live. The worry, the suspicion, the stress, the meanness. I keep dreaming that these dead are telling me what they would do if they could come back. What nobody has said so far: Rat out more folks and kick harder when asked.

Am I, like, a murderer? Are you? I think so, yes, wow.

Well, no life for me. Not up here, not down there.

So.

Don't mind dying but can't bear the thought of you helping, which, us being us, you pretty much would have to, I guess.

Hey, wow, look, I'm saving you again.

XO

A.

For Lunch, Shirley and Kiko send in steak, pudding, four Kit Kats, a milkshake. Plus a note: "Sorry re Amy. For the best, though painful. BTW: we feel you would make a fine Monitor. Appealing, we hope? Otherwise your outlook is grim. To be frank."

"Yes, please," I write at the bottom, and eat heartily, then send the note back on my cleaned plate.

But I will not become a Monitor.

Every day starts out as a certain day, dear reader, which, when it begins, we call today. Hence, every day, as we wake to a new today, we must assume that today may be the day. For what, though? That is what is unknown, that is what I must find out, and quickly now: for what will each of my coming todays henceforth be for?

I have Amy's letter, Rolph's letter. I have these notes I have written to you, dear reader.

Upon my release, I will rise, go to Copy Services, make Copies of these, go forth, leave Copies on every fake stump in the Room, every chair in Dining, in the Coat Check of DISCO, the stables of NOW WE JOUST, the saloons of WEST, on the seats of the Tram, as it speeds in its unceasing loop from sister workhouse to sister workhouse, from LOVEFEST, CALI CREEK, in the north, to DREAMY MAINE SUMMER, in the south, so that all may know the truth and be moved to ask, perhaps in some quiet moment: Is this world we have made a world in which lovers may thrive?

Though I will not live to see it, and dread the kicking that must come, may these words play some part in bringing the old world down.

MOTHER'S DAY

The trees along Pine Street that every spring bloomed purple flowers had bloomed purple flowers. So what? What was the big deal? It happened every spring. Pammy kept saying, "Look at the flowers, Ma. Ain't them flowers amazing?" The kids were trying to kiss up. Paulie had flown in and Pammy had taken her to Mother's Day lunch and now was holding her hand. Holding her hand! Right on Pine. The girl who once slapped her own mother for attempting to adjust her collar.

Pammy said, "Ma, these flowers, wow, they really blow me away."

Just like Pammy to take her mother to lunch in a sweatshirt with a crossed-out picture of a machine gun on it. What about a nice dress? Or pantsuit? At least this time Pammy and Paulie hadn't been on her about the smoking. Even back when Pammy was taking harp, even back when Paulie's hair was long and he was dating that Eileen, even after Eileen slept around and Paulie shaved his head, whenever Paulie and Pammy came over, they were always on her about the smoking. Which was rude. They had no right. When their father was alive they wouldn't have dared. When Pammy slapped her hand for adjusting her collar, Paul Sr. had given her such a wallop.

The town looked nice. The flags were flying.

"Ma, did you like your lunch?" Pammy said.

"I liked it fine," Alma said.

At least she didn't have an old-lady voice. She just had her same voice, like when she was young and nobody had looked better in a tight dress going for cocktails.

"Ma, I know what," Pammy said. "How about we walk up Pickle Street?"

What was Pammy trying to do? Cripple her? They'd been out two hours already. Paulie'd slept late and missed lunch. He'd just flown in and, boy, were his arms tired. Paul Sr. had always said that after a trip. Paulie had not said that. Paulie not having his father's wit. Plus, it looked like rain. Black-blue clouds were hanging over the canal bridge.

"We're going home," she said. "You can

drive me out to the grave."

"Ma," Pammy said. "We're not going to the grave, remember?"

"We are," she said.

At the grave she'd say, Paul, dear, everything came out all right, Paulie flew in and Pammy held my hand and for once they laid off the smoking crap.

They were passing the Manfrey place. Once, in the Nixon years, lightning had hit the Manfrey cupola. In the morning a portion of cupola lay on the lawn. She'd walked by with Nipper. Paul Sr. did not walk Nipper. Walking Nipper being too early. Paul Sr. had been a bit of a drinker. Paul Sr. drank a bit with great sophistication. At that time, Paul Sr. was selling a small device used to stimulate tree growth. You attached it to a tree and supposedly the tree flourished. When Paul Sr. drank a bit with great sophistication he made up lovely words and sometimes bowed. This distinguished-looking gentleman would appear at your door somewhat sloshed and ask, Were your trees slaggard? Were they gublagging behind the other trees? Did they need to be prodderated? And hold up the little device. In this way they had nearly lost the house. Paul Sr. was charming. But off-putting. In the sales sense. The efficacy of his tree stimulators was nebulous. Paul Sr. had said so in his low drunk voice on the night that it had appeared most certain they would lose the house.

"Mother," he'd said. "The efficacy of my tree stimulators is nebulous."

"Ma," Pammy said.

"What?" Alma snapped. "What do you want?"

"You stopped," Pammy said.

"Don't you think I know it?" she said. "My knees hurt. Daughter dragging me all over town."

She had not known it. She knew it now, however. They were opposite the shop where the men used to cut pipe. Which was now a Lean&Fit. The time they nearly lost the house, Paulie had come to their bed with a cup of pennies. He was bald these days and sold ad space in the *PennySaver*. Pammy worked at No Animals Need Die. That was the actual name. Place smelled like hemp. On the shirts and hats for sale were cartoons of cows saying things like "Thanks for Not Slamming a Bolt Through My Head."

And as children they'd been so bright. She remembered Paulie's Achievement Award. One boy had wept when he didn't get one. But Paulie'd got one. Yet they'd turned out badly. Worked dumb jobs and had never married and were always talking about their feelings.

Something had spoiled Paulie and Pammy. Well, it wasn't her. She'd always been firm. Once she'd left them at the zoo for disobeying. When she'd told them to stop feeding the giraffe they'd continued. She'd left them at the zoo and gone for a cocktail, and when she returned Pammy and Paulie were standing repentant at the front gate, zoo balloons deflated. That had been a good lesson in obedience. A month later, at Ed Pedloski's funeral, when, with a single harsh look, she'd ordered them to march past the open coffin, they'd marched past the open coffin lickety-split, no shenanigans.

Poor Ed had looked terrible, having been found after several days on his kitchen floor.

"Ma, you okay?" Pammy said.

"Don't be ridiculous," Alma said.

In the early days she and Paul Sr. had done it every which way. Afterward they'd lie on the floor discussing what colors to paint the walls. But then the children came. And they were bad. They cried and complained, they pooped at idiotic random times, they stepped on broken glass, they'd wake from their naps and pull down the window shades as she lay on the floor with

Paul Sr., not yet having done it any which way, and she'd have to rise, exasperated, which would spoil everything, and when she came back Paul Sr. would be out in the distant part of the yard having a minuscule perschnoggle.

Soon Paul Sr. was staying out all night. Who could blame him? Home was no fun. Due to Pammy and Paulie. Drastic measures were required. She bought the wildest underthings. Started smoking again. Once, she let Paul Sr. spank her bare bottom as she stood in just heels at the refrigerator. Once, in the yard, she crouched down, schnockered, waiting to leap out at Paul Sr. And leaping out, found him pantsless. That was part of it. The craziness. Part of their grand love. Like when she'd find Paul Sr. passed out on the porch and have to help him to bed. That was also part of their grand love. Even that time he very funnily called her Milly. One night she and Paul Sr. stood outside, at a window, drinks in hand, watching Paulie and Pammy wander from room to room, frantically trying to find them. That had — that had been in fun. That had been funny. When they finally went back in, the kids were so relieved. Pammy burst into tears, and Paulie began pounding Paul Sr. so fiercely in the groin

246

with his tiny fists that he had to be sent to —

Well, he certainly had not been sent to sleep in the garden shed in the dark of night. As he always claimed. They would not have done that. They had — probably they'd laughed it off. In their free-spirited way. Then sent him to bed. For hitting. After which, probably, he'd run out and hid in that shed. Rebelliously. They'd searched and searched. Searching and searching, heroically, they'd finally found him in the shed, sleeping naughtily across a fertilizer bag, tears streaking the dirt on his —

Why had he been crying when he was supposedly hiding rebelliously?

That was all a long time ago.

She wasn't getting in the fricking time machine about it.

Sky was black now over the library.

If Pammy got her caught out in the rain she would honest to God tear Pammy a new one.

One Fourth of July, Paul Sr. had groped her in the mums. He'd liked that. He'd been craving more wildness. Okay, pal, here it is. That did the trick. Around the time of the groping-in-the-mums one ceased hearing the name Milly, ditto Carol Menninger, ditto Evelyn Whoever. One briefly ceased hearing those names and smelling those

247

strange perfumes during that fleeting victorious period of victory-by-wildness. Where had the kids been, that magical Fourth of July? Somewhere happy with sparklers, probably. Two sparklers had approached. Then paused. Then departed pronto. Well, that would teach them to spy. That would teach them that adults needed their private time.

"Behold, kiddies," Paul Sr. had slurred drunkenly into her bare back. "Welcome to your painful eyeful."

Soon after that wild Fourth came another near-loss-of-house. All wildness ceased. In the absence of wildness, the names/perfumes resumed.

No. A person misremembered. They'd worked shoulder to shoulder to save the house, and the entire question of names/perfumes had permanently receded, both of them finding it humorous that anyone could possibly think that Paul Sr. would even consider —

She was so tired.

Stupid Pammy.

Inconsiderate Pammy.

"Home," she said.

Up ahead, across Pine, sweeping her walk — was that?

It was.

248

Debi Hather. Good God. Was she ever old.

The strange trashy girl in high school. Big hippie. Tiny head, curly hair, no chest. Look at her over there, still weird: Asian blouse, pants with ties at the ankles, bird-skinny. Who did she think she was, Gandhi or whoever? Mrs. Gandhi?

Hippie Grammy?

Sweeping like a banshee in front of that same tiny former carriage house she'd lived in since she was a girl. With her oddball parents. Mandy and Randy. Both had limps. Different limps. When they walked down the street it was like a freaking dance party.

Now, hang on a *briefen* short second there, Eisenstein, Paul Sr. said in her mind. Let's poise a hyperthetical: Say you were born to gimps, and grew up in a tiny house, and never had *und potten* to piss in? Mightn't you have turned out a strange lost gal with twelve or so marriages behind you and a tragic runaway daughter?

No, she answered. I wouldn't have.

You know that for a certainty? Paul Sr. said. Well, maybe I'm just dull. Perhaps I fail to grasp your immensely higher logic. Maybe, having lived a perfect life, you've got all the answers.

Don't.

Do not.

Do not defend that one there.

I merely pose the query, he said.

He was bearing down on her in that way of his, not even giving the other person a chance to —

Wong or white, snook? he said. Clock's ticking! Answer, please!

Well, how should she know? Who she'd be if she weren't her? Why would you want to even know that? It didn't amount to anything.

"Ma, you want to go over, say hi?" Pammy said. "She's an old friend, right?"

"Well, she's old," Alma said. "But she's no friend of mine."

"Ma, God," Pammy said.

"We never had nothing to do with her," Alma said. "Big hippie. Never meant nothing to us."

Not much.

Not much she hadn't.

Zowie! Here came Alma Carlson. Up Pine. Daughter in tow. Pammy or Kimmie or whoever. She'd seen the son, Paulie, at Wegmans yesterday, arms full of flowers. For Alma (!). Not sure how *that* worked: Mean Old Thing (Alma) gets Mother's Day flowers; Nice, Generous Mom (her, Debi) gets —

Lord, what a face: shriveled apple. Draw-string purse pulled tight.

When was God or whoever going to lower the boom? On a meanie like that? Or did she just get to live out her life, mean as all get-out? Oh God, Schmod, she, Debi, wasn't a big believer in God or Hell or any of that male-based crap. She'd been no angel herself, having done (yes) a few drugs in her day, and also she didn't exactly love the idea of showing up at the pearly gates or whatnot and having Saint Whoever look her up in his book and go: Whoa, hey, I was just sitting here tabulating the number of guys you had in your life, and, yikes, can you wait here a second while I go check with God on what the limit is?

Sweep, sweep.

(Why did we use that word when the actual sound was more like *swep*?)

Swep, swep.

Because, okay, yes, she'd loved men. And they'd loved her. Back in the day. For her? It was a form of joyous overflow. Like that art guy on TV who loved to paint so much that sometimes his wife got peeved, and he'd go, holding up his brush: "Joyous overflow, Joanie, mea culpa!" She'd been like that. But with sleeping with guys. Ha! She'd enjoyed every last one of them. Even

251

the sleazes. Especially the sleazes! That salesman from Indiana! With his little blindfolds? What had *that* been about! Did he carry them everywhere? Apparently! But God bless him, that was just *him,* that was his *thing.* Everyone had a thing, or several things, and her view was, if you loved the universe (which she did, or liked to think she did, or anyway sure *tried* to) you had to love *all of it.* Even Mr. Indiana (Ted? Todd?) with his little blindfold case. Where was he now? He'd been, like, fifteen years older than her. So he'd be . . . what? In a home? Dead? Having his own interesting conversation with Saint Whoever? Re the blindfolds? Re the not exactly stopping when she'd asked —

But even that — you learned something from everything. Or, at least, she did. What she'd learned from Mr. Indiana was —

Well, she wasn't sure.

Don't date guys from Indiana.

Ha.

What a hoot.

Swep.

Ted/Todd from Indiana had been followed by who? Whom? Carl, then Tobin, then the Lawrence/Gary combo. After that it got blurry. Lord, what a roster! She'd really lived. Had not discriminated between tall/

short, nerdy/cool, married/not married, whatever. No blockages. No hang-ups. If you're interested in me, I thank you for that, I bow to that part of you that bows to me, let's get it on. Ha. No, really, she recanted exactly *none* of it. Why recant openness to the moment? Bring it! Even now, bring it! Open, open, open! She ought to run across Pine and give Alma a hug. That would freak the old bitch out.

But no. If she'd learned anything in her life it was: You had to accept people the way they were.

Like Vicky. Her daughter. Whoever Vicky had been at any given moment, she, Debi, had accepted it. When Vicky wanted to be a bookworm and wear those big cloddy boots and memorize everything about the French Revolution and always be tidying up the house and scrubbing the toilets and what-not, she'd been like: Go for it, kiddo, I accept you. When Vicky wanted to mow the lawn because the parade was this weekend, and the whole town would see how long their grass was (as if *that* were a thing), have at it, *amiga,* even though you're only, like, eight, reach way up and dig in with your cloddy boots and push that big heavy mower, I won't be embarrassed about it at all.

Whatever Vicky had wanted to be, that had been fine with her.

Only wouldn't it have been cool if what Vicky had wanted to be was a less subservient, more out-there type of girl, so self-assured that nothing ever threw her? Somehow she'd gotten stuck with the wrong kid. Which made for some tension. Vicky was so *uptight.* Everything had to be *perfect.* Like once Vicky brought over this nice young guy, Dan, and she, Debi, made them mac and cheese, but there was no milk, as she'd been getting the runaround from Phil, or maybe it was Clive, and was a little distracted and hadn't been to the store in a week or two, so she made it with strawberry yogurt, and the kids declined to eat it, and she pointed out (just being honest) that they must be a couple of pretty privileged humans if they were turning up their noses at what would pass, in ninety percent of the world, for a fucking *feast,* and at the F-word Dan (the son of *surgeons*) had blanched or blushed or whatever and Vicky had started stuttering, and all that time, Vicky — she remembered this in particular, this detail being so classically *Vicky* (big self-sabotager) — had kept her *retainer* on, like a harmonica holder. With a boy over! What was *that* about?

So, yes: tense. Tense between them. Tenser and tenser. Finally, senior year, Vicky had pulled this really skillful tension-release move. Of bolting. Running off. With that little punk Al Fowler and his stringbean cousin. Al came back a few months later, said they'd left her in Phoenix, she was being a total bitch.

Two weeks after that, a postcard: "Ma, I'm fine, don't try find me."

And that was that.

Thirty-two years ago.

Not a word since.

Swep.

It was what it was.

But you know what? Actually? She felt good about it. She did. She'd raised an independent young woman. A warrior princess. A young woman so intent on getting what she needed she hadn't even bothered to say goodbye. To her own mother. That was bold. That was awesome. Because if Vicky *had* said goodbye, Debi would've tried to talk her out of it. She'd loved that kid so much. She would have said, like: Okay, look, agreed, I'm a mess, there are too many men in my life, I'm not always available to help you with — whatever, algebra or whatnot — but give me another chance, and I'll be more focused on *you* and

255

your needs, and will totally disavow who *I* am (a person always trying to say *yes* to life) and will do my best (hereby resolved!) to start saying *no* to life, and very fakely pouring myself into that constricting mold you seem to prefer me in ("Perfect Robotic Mother"), so that nothing I do will ever challenge you in the least or make you step even an inch outside your tiny restrictive comfort —

Alma was paused now across the street. Glaring at her. As if stuck.

What's up, kid? What do you want? A bow? A salute? A wave?

Here you go, pal.

Care to wave back, Your Majesty?

No?

Fine.

Far be it from her to judge. Anyone. At any time. To judge was to dominate. To place yourself above another. Which she refused to do. Some would. Many did.

Not her.

Although wouldn't it be a hoot when Alma kicked the bucket and Saint Whoever was like: Why so mean? Why so proud? Why such a hypocrite? Did you not find life beautiful? Where was your *heart*? Why did you squander your precious life force trying to possess, control, *interfere*?

256

And Alma, newly dead, would stand there, stunned, like: I'm having a realization right now. Who was correct? Debi. Who was wrong? Me, Alma. Then they'd show the movie of her life, and Alma would see what a fuckhound Paul had been and that would really drive it all home.

Would she, Debi, be standing nearby, inside Heaven, looking on, amused? No. Because she was going to outlive Alma.

Ha.

No. Let's say she was dead. She'd be like: I knew you in life, Alma. Do you remember me?

Gosh, Debi, hi, I do, Alma would say. And I am so sorry. I was always a super-snoot to you.

Yes, you were, she'd say. But I forgive you.

And Saint Whoever would look over, all impressed, like: Wow, even though she always treated you like crap, you are being totally cool to her right now.

But then again, you fucked my husband, Alma would say. Like, a gazillion times. According to that movie of my life I just now watched. Even when I was in the hospital having Pammy.

Does that come as a surprise to you? Saint Whoever would say. About your husband?

It does, yes, Alma would say. I lived in a

257

state of self-imposed blindness, never seeking truth.

That's too bad, Saint Whoever would say. That's some bad juju right there. What is the greater sin, do you think: adultery or standing in the way of true love?

I don't know, Alma would say.

Standing in the way of true love, Saint Whoever would say.

But he was my *husband,* Alma would say.

Well, marriage is just a shallow cultural tradition, Saint Whoever would say. At least, it is to us up here.

She fucked him and fucked him, Alma would say, all crest-fallen. Right under my nose. And I never knew.

And yet here I am in Heaven, Debi would say. Think about it.

Ha. That had all just popped out.

The creative mind, wow.

Especially hers.

Well, Paul had deserved better. Than Alma. He was so sweet. You got the feeling that, in being a fuckhound, he was just acting on his true nature. He took so much joy in it, flattered you so sincerely after, never ignored you in public, like so many did, but always lit up when he saw you and sometimes even gave you a wink, with Alma standing right there, which was weirdly delicious, because Alma (she had to admit it) had always had this sort of *glamour,* being one of the older girls and (oh, she could give her this much) really pretty. One time, at some sort of yard party, Paul had given Debi that wink and they'd snuck off to a pool shed or some such, and afterward, when he rejoined Alma, who was (as she so often was back then, ha ha) looking worried, Paul put his hand right on Alma's ass while giving her, Debi, a second wink, and Alma had brightened so sweetly at his hand on her ass, as if it really *meant* something to her, that, thinking of that pathetic little brightening now, she, Debi, felt a twinge of sisterhood, as in "Men are pigs, sister, are they not?," although, at the time, not so much, because she'd just been dumped by either Eric or Chase, and that second wink (which meant, as she took it, "*Das Wifen* has no clue how bondingly naughty it was for you to go down on me just now while sitting on that tub of chlorine") had just made her really, really happy.

Could that guy ever talk! "I am maximally ardent *pour toi,*" he'd said. She'd written that one down. In her Krazee Jernel. Those were the days! You did whoever, then wrote about it in your Krazee Jernel.

How could Alma not have known? What a

fucker Paul had been? Literally? Her, Linda, Milly K., that Iranian gal, both Porter sisters, Mag Kelly, Evelyn Sonderstrom. And those were just the ones she personally knew about! Everyone knew. How could Alma not know? You'd walk around town and there'd be tall pale nerdy Paul sneaking out of some house, or leading some gal (her, Debi, ha, guilty as charged) around the back of St. Jude's for a quickie, humming "Kumbaya" ironically. A few days after that, he'd sent her a bracelet. Nice bracelet, actually. Still had it. She should donate it. To a woman's shelter. Jesus, who had she *been* back then? Doinking a married guy? Behind a church?

No, you know what? She loved that woman. *Praised* that woman. That woman she'd been: authentic, spontaneous, never thought twice. About anything.

Just *leapt.*

Sometimes it was so frustrating! To have been born in the wrong time! In the future, she was pretty sure, people would be open and free, and fuck whoever they wanted, and live communally, all responsibilities shared, and if you dug cooking and cleaning and whatnot you'd do that, or if you were more creative, and felt more authentic hanging out with others, offering counsel re their problems, smoking a little hash to go deeper, you'd do that. Nobody would own anything or anyone. Everyone would do exactly what she or he liked, and nobody would gossip about anyone or look down on anyone or consider anyone slutty, and all of the houses would be exactly the same size, and if someone started to build some fancy addition, *bang,* everyone would be right there, going, *No you don't, we are all equal here,* and if the person made a fuss about it, they'd simply — well, there'd be some sort of council. That would very fairly and systematically bring that elitist down. To their level. Make her live in a smaller house. For penance. And some of that wiser subgroup who had chosen to give counsel and smoke hash might symbolically take over the oppressor's house. Just temporarily. And her husband. Until she was genuinely sorry. And if the elitist resisted, and refused to be genuinely sorry (as judged by them, the wiser subgroup), she could stay in that much smaller house until she relented, while the wiser group gathered outside, taunting her, enacting a sort of virtuous blockade, until she was nearly dying of hunger and —

It was so unfair. She'd loved Paul and Paul had loved her, but she'd never gotten to live with him for even a single minute, and then he'd broken it off, and she'd had to drive by his house every day on her way to that stupid receptionist job, watching that ugly new addition go up (and up and up), and sometimes there'd be Alma, standing cross-armed amid the framing, smugly smoking.

And yet.

Who'd triumphed? Who was happy? Who was happy right now? Was Alma? She didn't look very happy.

She, Debi, was happy.

Happy in this moment, just as it was. Wind picking up, clouds dark over the Rec, left heel out of her slipper: all perfect.

Game, set, match: Debi.

Life was harsh, people said. But no. She disagreed. Life was wise. Life *compensated.* The love of your life broke it off, and many years passed, and your kid ran off, and that about killed you, but then, laid low, you were forced to take stock, see what had been good in your life, see what had been best, and when your answer was "Paul, Paul was the best thing that ever happened to me," you drifted back to him, sought him out, sort of lured him back into it, into you, and what did you get? The happiest year of your life. Of both your lives. He said so. "I've never been so happy. That's the truth." His exact words. So she had that. Then he died. Just her luck.

She couldn't exactly show up at Chasen-Winney for visiting hours, so she'd snuck out to the grave a few days later, bawling her eyes out. Then here came Alma. As always. The Interferer, the Truncator. In that sweet red Granada that Paul had just bought her. For her birthday. Ouch. Off she, Debi, had scurried, through the woods, ruining her new black pumps, because (who knew?) there was a *swamp* back there, eventually stumbling out, like some sort of dispirited ghost, at Wendy's, where she'd had a milkshake, clay-red mud pooling around her wrecked shoes, that mopping kid looking over at her, like: Lady, it's weird that you're crying in Wendy's. Please leave, so I can clean your shit up.

And then she'd had to call Cal from work to drive her back to the graveyard to get her Dart.

The end.

Alone ever since.

Swep.

"Ma, jeez, wave back," Pammy said. "You're acting nuts."

I don't believe I will, Alma thought.

"She's just some old lady," Pammy said.

263

"Why hurt her feelings? Anyways, that's what I think."

"That's because you don't know shit about anything," Alma said. "Look at you. What have you ever done?"

The breeze was suddenly cold, and leaves were skittering around.

Oh, great. Now Pammy was mad. Boohoo. Pammy was touchy. Dainty. Who knew why? She'd always treated Pammy-Putt square.

Ha. Pammy-Putt. She'd almost forgotten they used to call her that. Pammy-Putt. With the pigtails. At the end of one pigtail a pink tie and at the end of the other a yellow. Because Pammy-Putt wanted it like that. Little Pammy-Putt, standing on the footstool, confidently directing the pigtailing. She hadn't thought of that in — she could smell that kid's head now. Sort of sweet. Cloverish. Where had that smell gone? Where had that confident little gal —

Once Pammy-Putt came home from second grade asking what a *laughingstock* was. And what was a *philanderer*? Who'd said those things? Alma demanded. Who'd been telling those filthy lies? She'd had a few nips. So was forceful. Pammy wouldn't cough up a name. So she'd had Pammy stand on one foot awhile. Then Pammy-Putt got her mouth good and scrubbed with soap for disobeying a direct —

The church bells at St. Caspian's rang once, twice, three times.

Now here came the rain. Perfect. Stupid Pammy. Eight blocks from home. Her knees were shot. What's the plan, Pam? You carrying me? Pammy had a bad back. Pammy wasn't carrying shit.

Some little hail thingies came bouncing up off the sidewalk.

Pretty.

Ouch. Not pretty.

Hey! Damn! What the —

"Ma, we better run for it," Pammy said.

Run? You run. I can't, dummy, I haven't run in —

Then she was. Running. Kind of. Behind Pammy. God, the shuffling funny way they ran now. The hail stung her arms like wasps. Wasps coming straight down. A lemon-sized hail thingie smashed on the sidewalk in front of them like a sno-cone.

Holy crap, if that hit a person?

Pammy had her sweatshirt off now and was holding it up. Over Alma's head. Lord, what a kid. Standing there in her bra, bare pink arms up. So her ma wouldn't get zoinked. Hair full of the smaller-sized hail thingies, like the plastic beadlets on them old Catholic —

She felt a rush of tenderness for Pammy.

Something clipped Pammy in the head and a red mini-divot appeared at her hairline. Pammy seemed stunned. Too stunned to move. A tree? By the Obernicks'. She pushed Pammy over by the tree. That was better. No, it wasn't. The hail was cutting right down through the branches now. A shower of snapped branches crashed down on the Obernicks' fence: one, two, three-fourfive. Jesus, they had to get out of here. One more branch came down, caught her on the shoulder. Hey, that hurt, clown! Like the time Karl Metz had whacked her with that hammer.

Someone was calling her name.

From across the street.

The hail thingies bouncing off Debi's black umbrella looked like sweat flying off a cartoon guy's head when he was supposed to be worried. Paul Sr. had once shown her a porn like that. A cartoon porn. The one Paulie later found. Guy so worried, watching his wife have at it with a big sailor or —

It wouldn't do. Wouldn't do having Debi help. Or would it? It might. It wouldn't. Paul had liked that one too much. Of all of them, he'd liked her best and stayed at her longest and gone back to her way after all the others were done. It was humiliating. That he should stay longest with the trashiest, strangest of all, always speaking kindly of her, as if he actually might —

Old man. Stupid old man. Old man in love. Old man so happy, in his boxers, in front of the fan, telling her all about it, like she was supposed to be happy, happy for him, happy for —

She waved Debi off.

We don't need you, slut. We won't have you.

She leaned against the Obernicks' fence. Dirty fence. Someone should paint it.

"Ma?" Pammy said, trickle of blood running down her face. "You okay? Ma?"

She pushed Pammy off. She couldn't breathe. When pushed off, Pammy stayed off. Pammy was like that. Sweet but weak. No bounceback. You could push her right off.

The fence gave way. The ground came up. Ouch. Cheap fence. She ought to sue those stupid Ober —

She was on the ground now, severed bike pedal huge in her sight, ant crawling along it. The fence was up. Still up. Hadn't given way. Only she had. Why the hell was she on the ground?

Oh God, something with her heart, something with her —

The church bells at St. Caspian's rang once, twice, three times.

Rain coming. What a drag.

She'd be stuck inside all day.

Across Pine, the Denisons' sunflowers were bending in the breeze. Alma and what's-her-name were standing hunched over like a couple of lady trolls. Mom troll and daughter troll, out on the troll town. On Troll Mother's Day. How nice. How sweet. How weird.

One last *swep.*

Here it came.

Let it rain! Jesus, what a deluge! Bring it! Yes! Gorgeous! Memo from Mother Nature: I can be one crazy dame. Don't piss me off, I shall instantaneously make Pine Street a river and back up the gutters and cast forth (whoa! dang!) a torrent of tiny pinging crystals, which you humans call "hail," but which I, Mother Nature, call "my wondrous display," which shall resound or rebound to the music I play, such that they shall — whoa, dang, fuck! — ricochet up off the rain-slick black street and come bouncing back as high as your waist, falling alike on the lowly and the —

Walnuts!

Golf balls!

Sheesh!

Damn!

How was Alma doing over there? Not great. Getting pounded. Ha! There you go, kid. There's an example of world-serving-as-teacher. Try snooting your way out of this one, Your Majesty.

From somewhere came the sound of a parade, that distant-drum sound, which was weird, because wouldn't any parade have been canceled? On account of the hail? Only it wasn't a parade; it was the sound the biggest hailstones yet made smashing down on (yikes!) the Obernicks' Fiesta, the Neillys' trash can, which — oof! — tumped over (as if knocked unconscious) and rolled out onto Pine.

Pammy or Cammie or whoever had her shirt off and was making a tent of it, over Alma.

Over her mother.

Kind of sweet, actually.

Oh, hell's bells, hang on, somewhere in this mess she must have a —

She stepped in, grabbed Dad's duck-handled umbrella from the rack, stepped out.

Because who was she? She was Debi. Who was Debi? Debi was generous, a generous soul. She was known for that — she gave and gave and reached out to others, no matter how badly they'd treated her, even a meanie like Alma, who (yes, okay, she admitted it) she'd often wished dead, so that she might have a decent chance at the man she loved and a real house and all the things you were supposed to get in this world — but, no, she didn't wish Alma dead anymore, because she, Debi, was *love,* was *forgiveness,* was *goodness,* was *light;* where there was need there was Debi, which was why she was about to do what she was about to —

She stepped out, umbrella up, yelled across.

Wait.

Wait a minute.

Had Alma waved her off?

She had. Oh my God. You have got to be kidding. What nerve! What balls! Still queen? Peasant girl still too lowly? To come fetch you, Your Highness?

Stick it, Alma.

Let this be a lesson to you.

There is some shit I will not eat.

Because she, Debi, was also a person who had the wisdom to let the world teach the evil ones a lesson while she stood calmly by, watching/trusting the cosmos.

270

She stepped back inside, slammed the door, shot the umbrella down into the stand, retreated to the middle room, Mom and Dad's old room, angrily pulled her tax things from the file cabinet, sat shuffling the forms uselessly around, thinking of how strange it was (beautiful, really, a mysterious unsought blessing) that after a lifetime of being everybody's joke (easy lay, jilted lover, discarded mom), she was finally (in the eleventh hour) learning to frigging stand up for herself.

She stayed in there about fifteen minutes, fuming, getting absolutely nothing done, until she heard the first ambulance arrive and leapt to the window, heart in her throat, and watched as, without even trying the shock paddles, they pulled the sheet up over Alma's head and loaded her in.

Debi's mind lurched forward, sputtered, went quiet.

Alma got hold of a fence slat. To pull — pull herself out. Of this. Pain. Something new was happening now. The tightness in her chest was worse. Jesus. Like labor with Paulie. Then it went past that, to labor with Pammy, and she was giving birth to something bigger than Pammy, out her chest.

God oh God.

271

Pop! is how she would have described it had she still been able to describe.

Pop!

A number of little beings came now. God, get back. You didn't know whether to pet them or kick them. As they gazed at her intently, she saw they were saying: *Careful, girlie, careful.*

Then their boss-being came: a man.

Paul Sr.

Looking so handsome.

"Did you finally wake up, dear?" she said. "And love the right person? The one who knew you longest and understood you best?"

Looking at him, she saw the answer was no.

Still no.

The many little beings condensed down into just two. A boy and a girl. Paul tapped them on the head and they turned into babies. Who stood cowering beside Paul. Giving her the stink eye. Like he was guarding them. From what? From her? In a pig's ass! It was his fault! He never let us be a family!

"Now will you accept me as I am?" Paul said.

What? What a crock! How about you accept *me* as *I* am? Treat me nice. Like a wife.

A real wife. Is that too much to ask? Forsake all others. Love just *me*. Will you? Will you?

She saw it was still a no and always would be.

It hurt. So much. Again. Well, if he wanted a fight, she knew how to fight. She liked it. She was good at it. She'd make him pay. The way she always had. You'd think he'd know that by —

She looked down. Her hands were glowing. Glowing red.

"This has nothing to do with him," the girl baby said. "How do *you* want to be?"

How could that baby talk so well? She was like a little genius. In a diaper. And what did she mean? It had everything to do with him. He'd done it all. Turned everything bad. Before Paul had messed with her, she'd been a smiling little dear sniffing lilacs on graduation day, swinging her diploma by one corner. It was Paul. Paul who'd made her hands this way. She went to wipe her eyes and started her hair on fire.

No problem.

Didn't hurt.

Much.

Now Paul was gone. The babies looked lost. She should pick them up. She went for the boy. His eyes got wide at her hot hands. He toddled away. She went for the girl. She toddled away. It was like when you dropped a piece of paper on a windy day and it grew a mind bent on eluding you. She stood still. The babies drifted back. They wanted her. But she had the hand problem. She went for the boy. Who toddled away. She went for the girl. Who toddled away.

Then it happened again.

And again.

For like a hundred years.

A stump appeared. At some point.

At least now she could sit.

She sat, trying to figure it out.

It seemed she was meant to admit that she was wrong. But she wasn't. If she was wrong about this, there was no right.

Maybe she could fake it.

"Okay, okay," she said aloud. "I was wrong. The whole time. About everything."

Hands still hot.

The stump began rising. Lifting her above the babies. Then: a terrible bark-cackling. The other beings were back. With big old teeth.

Here they came, scrambling hyena-like across a vast plain.

Real baby-eaters.

Lord, so fast. She'd have to hoist the babies up. She reached down, grabbed the boy, singed his little arm.

274

How to do it, how to do it, how to get her hands to cool?

"Whose fault was it?" the girl baby asked.

"His!" Alma cried. "His, his, his!"

Her arms went hot right up to the elbows. Big bully! Whoever'd made her this way, unable to lie, was jerking her around now because she wouldn't lie.

The hyena-beings were closing in, all meat-breath and yellow teeth.

"Whose?" the girl baby said. "Whose fault?"

"I don't know," she cried desperately. "I'm sorry, I'm sorry, I really don't! Mine? My fault?"

"No," the girl baby said.

What the hell? Fine, forget the babies, she'd keep the hot hands. She was what she was. No one could blame her. As long as she was Alma, she'd be mad. She had a right. Did she *want* to be mad? No. What she wanted to be was her, younger. Her, non-mad. Her, not yet mad. Pre-Paul. Smelling lilacs, swinging that diploma. No, even before that: so young she wanted nothing yet, liked nothing, disliked nothing. No, before that: before she was even Alma, because Alma would always find Paul, love Paul, and Paul would always be Paul.

It came to her, and then was happening: it

would be fixed when she stopped being Alma.

Her arms and hands went cool and pale, perfectly normal.

She reached down, hauled the babies up.

"Who do you *want* to be?" the girl baby whispered into her ear as the stump rose just high enough to keep them safe from the hyena-beings bark-cackling below.

It was like waiting at the top of the Alpine in that little wooden car, unable to believe that what was about to happen was about to happen, and then, even as you thought, God, oh God, this cannot possibly —

"Nobody even close to home in there," the paramedic named Henry said to the paramedic named Claire.

Which was rude, Claire thought. But, actually, no, it was fine: the daughter was out of earshot, sobbing against a tree.

ELLIOTT SPENCER

Today is to be Parts of the Parts of my

Sure, Jer Please do Point at parts of me while saying the name of it off our list of Words Worth Knowing.

Agespot

Finger

Wrist

At *wrist* Jer says: This one's been broken, seems like.

Then pokes.

Ouch? he says.

Yes, I say.

Groin

Waist

You were no spring chicken, says Jerry.

I do not understand what you just said, please explain, I say.

You were not young, Jerry says. Your body is not the body of a young person.

Oh, that's cool, I say. That's cool, Jer.

Jer shakes his head his certain way Meaning: 89, you crack my ass up.

Long ago, perhaps one week, we had Explain Time, due to figure of speech *crack my ass up* All asses are *precracked,* turns out, even mine, which Jer helped me learn by taking of *phonephoto.*

Arm

Leg

Navel

Scar, on *Stomach*

Penis

All morning we continue learning and learning until no part of me remain.

And at night all night as every night a tape playing in here helps improve me our Syntax.

Have we done *bellow*? Jer says.

Makes loud startling sound.

Now you, Jer says.

I *bellow.*

So, what we are going to be bellowing *at*? Jer says. Whoever is standing across from us.

Whoever is standing across from us, I say.

Feel free to bellow words or phrases, he says.

HELLO! I bellow.

You are always so good at everything, 89, he says.

Then pours into me, so generous, by saying them, some words I may wish to bellow:

Bastard

Turd

Creep

Idiot

May we do Defining? I say.

Uh, sure, Jer says.

Turns out, all mean same:

Bastard = individual standing across from us.

Turd = individual standing across from us.

Creep = individual standing across from us.

Idiot = individual standing across from us.

89, I have always so far called you 89, Jer says. But tomorrow you are to become Greg. How's that?

I am Greg? I say.

Will be, Jer says. Tomorrow. Because tomorrow is, guess what? Job One Day.

Exciting! Have been waiting long for Job One Day Job One turns out per Jer is: *high and noble as all getout* Per Jer: I will stand for *freedom* For *poor* and *sick* Will defend *weak* From *oppressors.*

279

More Defining, with help of HandiPics:

Freedom = cartoon bird flies above land, smile on beak.

Poor = sad child, pockets sticking out of pants.

Sick =thin guy in bed, X's for eyes.

Weak = guy in desert, trying to reach water glass, failing.

Oppressor = tall guy with monster face sticks stick into body of *weak* as, in four HandiPics in row, *weak* gets more *weak* with each poke.

Why do *oppressors* wish to poke *weak*? I say.

They're bad, says Jer. Have to be stopped.

From doing that, I say.

Correcto, says Jer. And you're a big part of the solution.

What the what! as Jer might say.

Never have I felt being me to be so worth it so far.

Job One Day!

Bus, Jer says. *Cohort.*

Cohort = many new pals on *bus* All, like me, in greens.

Rumbling and we move.

Talk among yourselves, Jer says.

We do We do so Each of us say our names I say mine of Greg That one is Larry That one is Vince So is that one And that one And that one This one is Greg like me As is that one That one, Greg also So is that one Greg, near the front Here is Conor Seven Conors in all Eight Williams All happy Except Jer.

Jer, on phone: Hey, nice naming, Roberta. And that was your one damn job.

Cranky, I say. Crankypants.

Guess what, 89, Jer says softly You talk better than any of these other galoots.

True: my *cohort* speaks rather baby, somewhat lowly.

Because of you, Jer, I say.

Rumbling ends.

Ready, pal? Jer says. To bellow?

Hope so, I say.

Jer and other equal Supervisors lead us To: *trees* But something wrong: Our *tree,* in our HandiPic, has *squirrel* No squirrel at all near these *trees*! They better fix our Handi-Pic!

Supervisors say, Take off greens Fold and leave here Then give us new of various colors I look at ourselves naked with a rather shyness Having only previous seen own *penis, groin, gut* in own Room Valiant mirror We dress quickly Follow Jer and Supervisors down *hill* Small white flowers bob as we Say, I have not walked this far in Well, ever!

There they are, Jer says.

And yes there they So many *Bastards, Turds, Creeps, Idiots* standing across from us Between them and us: long low area I would term: *river* Filled not with water though but *Police* looking nervous.

I feel shy being first to bellow but love Jer so much I just bellow.

Others join Gregs, Conors, Williams, Vinces All join Bellowing until our throat actually hurts.

BastardTurdCreepIdiot! one Conor bellows.

What a creative way to He just runs them all togeth

Do we ever stand for *sick* and *poor,* defend *weak* from *oppressors*! By bellowing at those *BastardTurdCreepIdiot*! Across that approximate Police *river*! O small white flowers underfoot O in each five *tree* tops, birds Sometimes a small branch will drop As if sung down By bird.

Well done, Jer says on bus. Really good job, everybody.

Greens brought back and we re-dress.

Get ready, Jer says.

Then it is *Root Beer* Which I have never None of us has Suddenly in love with *Root*

Beer and would like another Can we? We may.

All the way home, warm happy *Root Beer* blur.

Jer looks over gives wink of: 89, you did good.

Which sure of course will well one's heart.

Room Valiant has *intercom problem* A crackle will come All in Room Valiant may then clearly hear who are out there talking, while they, out there talking, do not know it.

Once, for example, long ago, last week, Kennedy B., talking on phone to boyfriend Kevin:

I shop, I cook, said Kennedy B. Plus I have a job I actually have to, like, *go* to?

Meg, there with me and Jer in Room Valiant, gave Jer look of: Ha, we are hearing Kennedy B. on phone and she does not know it. Then put finger to lips, meaning: If quiet, will hear more.

That is not work, Kevin, Kennedy B. said. I do not consider letting Jeeves in and out actual work. When someone starts sending you a check for that, or for scooping its poop, that is a job. In my view.

We should probably get that thing fixed, Meg said.

Oh, gosh, said Kennedy B. Is that on? Can you guys hear me?

No, Jer said.

I'm not talking to you, babe, Kennedy B. said. I'm talking to Jerry and Meg.

Today, me alone in Room Valiant, here comes same crackle:

Here's what I don't get, Meg says. Why does he need *agespot*? Why *precracked*? Right? Big waste. He just needs to know enough so we can move his old ass around. Are we making butlers up in here? Substitute hubbies for widows? Are we back to that?

I wish, Kennedy B. says sad ly.

Honestly? says Jer. It floats my boat. This shit gets pretty boring.

Butlers? Hubbies? Widows? Floats? Boat? Shit?

I did not understand what you just said, please explain, I say.

89, did you hear all that just now? says Jer.

Yes, I say.

Go to sleep, 89, Meg says. Big day tomorrow.

Job Two tomorrow, Jer says. You've been approved for Job Two.

Because of how good you did on Job One, says Meg. Isn't that great?

You're really going places, 89, says Kennedy B.

Job Two:

Again *bus.*

Arrive at whole new *Site.*

Some ladies step out from separate *bus* For them to change behind: *scrim* Which our Supervisors term: *unfortunate scrim* While doing mad winking Ladies go in green and come out in clothes of various One cannot get shoe on and smiling at self shakes head, tosses shoe Takes off other shoe, tosses As if to say, *Oh heck, who needs shoes to bellow?*

We men enter *unfortunate scrim* Which still smells somewhat lady ish Here are the ladies' green clothes heaps All freeze, our eyes go a little blank Break it up, says Jer, alarm ed.

Dream on, says Supervisor Marty.

Like that's happening, says Jer.

And thrusts into our arms clothes bundles anew.

Today I am: white sweater blue pants floppy tan hat.

Seen through bouncing walking heads of our cohort: *playground* Like its HandiPic Except not Another wrong HandiPic! This *playground* has no *children* chasing *butterfly*!

Only *Police* Standing unhappy One sitting in *swing* His *Police* friend gives him a stick-poke Which hops him to his feet While his *swing* just *swings* He who hopped looks at me direct I try a wink.

No go.

That *Police* must not feel like winking.

Beyond *Police:* big crowd of *Bastard-TurdCreepIdiots.*

We bellow What loudness for good we make! Then something occurs One *Bastard-TurdCreepIdiot* suddenly is over here On our side Among us! Bellowing! At us! So close I can see his sore on lip The quietest Greg gives him a slap He slaps quiet Greg right back Our largest Vince moves a fist to face of *BastardTurdCreepIdiot BastardTurd-CreepIdiot* goes down No longer bellowing Just covering face Ducking down meek Several Williams, a slim Conor, three Vinces gather rough around him Their feet and legs start going.

Say that must that must really

I withdraw Breathing hard Here is a small bathroom house That really smells like it I sit inside against one of its wall Heart leaping in bad manner Is brief rest fine during Job?

Hope so.

Here comes Jer.

What the hell are you doing in here, 89? he says. Jesus, come on.

Greg, I say.

Greg, right, sure, whoever, says Jer.

Dragged, by Jer, past *water fountain* Which runs on and Though no one drinking from Past three baby *trees,* wired to ground Pushed by dear Jer back over with my

Hoo boy.

My Conors Gregs Vinces my

Good old Jer.

Kudos, Jer.

No *Root Beer* for me thanks on way home. Because of *crying.*

I know *crying* I just have never done it.

I *cry* and *cry.*

Jer, softly, close to me: What are you do-ing, 89, why are you crying?

Me: I don't know, sorry, sorry.

Jer: Stop. You need to stop. Do you see anyone else on this bus crying?

No, I say.

Kicking Conor and the kicking Williams and kicking-punching Vinces are just hap-pily drinking *Root Beer.*

Take this, Jer says.

Gives me a small white bit of

Jer you always have my back Jer Thank you Jer You do not want my *cohort* to see me *crying* And I do not want my *cohort* to

287

see me *crying* too.

Eat, he says. Eat it, dummy. You can't just hold it. It's a *pill.* Eat it.

Mere secs later don't feel sad At all Though face still wet, I feel pretty pretty darn good And sleepy Pretty darn good pretty darn sleepy.

If slumping down and with left eye look out *window:*

Nighttime *farms* fly by.

Why must all nighttime *farm* windows be orange? is a sweet mystery to think upon as down to sleep you

Must be night as heat is on.

Feel like taking sweaty greens off.

Do so.

Start again *crying* Why *crying* again? That kicking that kicking that punching That darn *Beatdown.*

That word springs into my

Just like snap.

And just like snap I know *beatdown* is: kickingkickingpunching in *alley.*

What the what! As Jer might say From where did that?

And just like snap I know *alley* is: wet black floor outside, with *music* coming from back of:

Tom's Dizzy Oasis.

Music Ha! *Tom's Dizzy Oasis* Ha ha!

To who did *beatdown* happen? To whom? To whom did *alley beatdown* to *music* behind *Tom's Dizzy Oasis* happen to?

Me, I say. Greg.

No, I say.

89? I say.

No, I say.

Silence Room Valiant does its usual *Hum clack-clock* Then a sound like something medium just dropped off table Although nothing did.

Elliott Spencer, I say.

Hum clack-clock Hum clack-clock.

Elliott Spencer Elliott Spencer, I say.

Jer comes in Bearing breakfast.

89, Christ, put some clothes on, he says.

Elliott Spencer, I say.

Jer drops breakfast.

In come Meg and Kennedy B.

You're not in trouble, 89, says Meg.

Hope not, I say.

Smells like OJ in here, says Kennedy B.

But who is Elliott Spencer? says Meg.

Me, I say. Was. Was me.

Was when? says Kennedy B. Was you when?

Before, I say.

Jer: Eyes go wide Taps *knuckle* on table

289

once two three.

Before when? says Kennedy B.

Before I came here, I say. In *van.*

Yikes, says Meg.

And you were there, I say to Jer.

Look on Jer's face says: If still holding breakfast, would drop it again.

Per Meg we hasty redo my *Scrape Test.*

In which Jer runs by me some words Do I know them or in the slightest recall:

Schenectady   NO
Coleman Street Bridge   NO
Reverend Barry Knox   NO

There you go, Jer says. Clean.

I don't know, says Meg. Freaks me out. The name? The van? Freaks me out.

We need forty, Jer says. Do we have forty?

We have thirty, says Meg. Counting 58 and 31.

Don't count 58 and 31, says Kennedy B.

58 can't take the simplest directive, says Meg.

And God forbid someone asks 31 a frigging question, says Kennedy B.

Meg: Maybe let's don't do this in front of —

By which she means me.

89's cool, Jer says. Right, 89?

Hope so, I say.

And I do hope so I am cool for sake of Jer Good old Jer! Kudos, Jer Who leaves behind own family every morning deep in *Burbury Estates* Sandi, Ryan, Little Jerry, baby Flint Who each night they await your return As each morning I await your return Jer who in early times my brain so *blankslate* all I could say was *blegblegbleg* taught me word upon word in his good firm impatient voice in Room Valiant with his sometimes macaroni breath.

Pal means *friend.*

Who is my one and only *pal, friend,* in world so far?

Jer and Jer alone.

Today is: Job Three Per Jer: *Real biggie.*

Real biggie = more big than anything yet in terms of our standing for *poor* and *sick,* defending *weak* from *oppressors.*

Job Three Site is in wild grass *field* Where, per Jer, *Indians* once started up *there,* on hill, then swept whooping down, past *here.*

Up there, now (from where, long ago, *Indians* started down): *ChickenFuego.*

I could go for some of that, says Supervisor Marty.

More *BastardTurdCreepIdiots* than ever before Jer nervous Marty nervous All Supervisors nervous *Police* nervous.

Hey, check this out, says Marty. Is that a frigging arrowhead?

Bends to get.

Ugh, stupid regular rock, says Marty

Throws at *phonepole.*

Uh-oh, says Jer.

Suddenly two *BastardTurdCreepIdiots* Arms joined as one Come flying through *Police* Into us Are among us.

Punch goes the Vince with the long hair Kick goes him and two Conors A Vince with short hair gives a kick Soon a crowd is around those down-punched down-kicked two Here comes three additional to rescue their More Gregs and Vinces and Conors rush over Soon their rescue men need rescue One rescue man is a true fighter Too bad for him To stop his fighting takes So many punches and kicks that Soon no way is he getting up Or fighting Or moving At all.

Some *ChickenFuego* folks on break look down upon us, hands on heads, as if they find our fighting amazing.

What a clusterfuck, Jer says.

Eek, shit, cameras, says Marty.

Coming down former *Indian* hill: Line of men and ladies with, I guess, *cameras?* Their *cameras* different from *camera* in our HandiPic Which is to be held in one hand By smiling *grandma* pointing it at *moose* in *canyon.*

Why is it all them over here, and us beating them up? says Jer. Why can't we get a few of us over *there,* and them beating *us* up?

Good question, says Marty.

All across the world, country, whatever, who right now looks like the bad guy? says Jer.

We do, says Marty.

Longhair Vince wanders out from the fighting.

Jer: Vince, hey, buddy. Up for a challenge? Fun challenge?

Vince drops into weary sit Looking down at one red hand Like red glove.

Poor Jer My *pal* Woke happy today But no Job Three, *real biggie* is now *clusterfuck* My sad *pal* Does so much for all with his so many *worries at home* such as: Sandi about to *leave his sorry ass* for Terence, *New Age douche* at her work unless Jer gets some *shorter work hours going pronto.*

I place myself so Jer's eyes may find me.

89! Jer says. Greg!

Jer comes close, voice goes soft.

I need you to do me a solid, 89, Jerry says. Will you? For the Job? For me? For Meg, for Kennedy B.?

For you, I say.

■ ■ ■ ■

Over I go Between two *Police*

Where's that old fart think he's going? shouts one.

Over there! I say.

Then am among *BastardTurdCreepIdiots* Bellowing *Bastard, Turd, Creep,* bellowing *Idiot.*

Heads turn Eyes go: Why so rude?

Then come fists Once I am good and down: kicks Ouch Ouch Everything going as planned Jer, please see please see my *beatdown* Then this *beatdown* starts reminding of from long-ago times other *beatdowns* Such as:

Elliott Spencer, under *bridge* Just like snap his money he got from returning *shit tons of empties* Is gone Who took? *Grady! Grady* brought *wine* After *wine, Grady* held rock Gave wink Then: wham *Damn you, Grady You took my damn*

Asleep after, pebble under hip O aching head O so blotto, sleep through whole thunderstorm *Everyone against me Always All my life Not fair Not my fault Tomorrow better borrow some bucks from Sal if I can trick that dumb bitch* Morning and O aching head Wake up wet from rain The place to poop is near the old fridge *O, please, wine.*

The kicks and punches keep ouch ouch
Coming

In memory: from Skanky Trey and his
fuckbuddy, Len From Rhett, boyfriend of
Sylvia From three rich kids and their short-
skirt gals One of who pours a drink down
on me: (Here drunk, she says drunken ly.
Have a drink, drunk

Laughlaughlaughs from the other short-
skirts.)

The kicks and punches also keep ouch
ouch coming In real life: from tightening
chanting crowd of *BastardTurdCreepIdiots.*

Ouch ouch ouch.

Through my fingers catch redglimpse of
Jer Pushing guy with *camera* near, so *camera* will see and show What needs to be seen
and I guess shown?

Then comes so much real-life *beatdown* I
put head down with eyes closed and hands
over ears so as not to hear the thump, crack,
ouch of it all.

You are the man, says Jer.

Hope so, I say.

Then open my one eye that still can.

Am not in Room Valiant At all Cat hops
uptop fancy book pile.

As you seem to be noting, 89, Meg says,

295

this is not Room Valiant.

That cat? says Kennedy B. Your cat.

Those pictures, on that bookshelf? says Meg. You, when young.

Meant to be you when young, says Kennedy B.

This is a rental, we rented it, says Jer.

And created those pictures using Face-Blend, says Meg.

I love this one, says Kennedy B. You look so happy to be hunting.

With your son, says Meg.

Greg Jr., says Jer.

It's like a game, Meg says. We're playing that, all along, all your life, this has been your home. Greg's home. Cool, right?

89, have we done *wino*? says Jer.

Jer shows HandiPic for *wino*: Guy in smushed *tophat,* X's for eyes, red cheeks, lying on side under lamp pole, fancy man in not-smushed *tophat* steps over him, holding own nose.

So, I'm just going to say it? Jer says. That was you. Most of your life. Spent a lot of time shitfaced down by the river. No kids, no wife, hadn't worked in fifteen years. In and out of jail. Big *wino. Disgusting *drunk.*

Who wants to be that guy? says Meg. You know? I mean, good riddance.

To bad riddance, says Kennedy B.

What a victory, though, right, when you think of it? says Jer. Old worthless *wino* who, in his life, did a lot of regrettable things, was a burden to all? Now, late in the game, gets a chance to start doing some pretty wonderful things?

Even on a national basis? says Kennedy B.

Do you have any idea how many people all over the country watched you get your butt beat the other day? says Meg.

Two million, says Kennedy B. As of noon.

Two million folks, looking afresh at our cause, says Meg. What a blessing. For the movement.

For which we work, says Kennedy B.

By whom we are contracted, says Jer.

In which we very much believe, says Meg.

Anyhoo, says Kennedy B.

Onward to Job Four, says Meg.

My eye goes wide.

Oh, poor sweetie, no, Kennedy B. says. No more fighting. You're done with all that.

Job Four is going to be you lying right here, says Meg. As you are.

Sitting up, if possible, says Kennedy B.

Talking to a nice lady curious about you and your life, Meg says.

Your life as Greg, says Jer.

You are Greg, will continue to be Greg, a simple nice old guy who, having retired from a life of teaching math at a local community college, grew sad watching your country go in all the wrong directions and, as a sort of late-life hobby or attempt to pay back all that was given to you by this wonderful nation, became active in politics and, accordingly, felt, and still do feel, compelled to join these protests in order to let your feelings be known, says Kennedy B.

We may want to go a little simpler with that, says Jer.

And if I touch my hat, act sick, says Meg. Excuse yourself, get up, go to the bathroom.

Does he even know where the bathroom is? says Kennedy B.

I'll be wearing a hat, Meg says to me. Then. At that time.

Plus can he walk? says Kennedy B.

KTOD's here in ten, says Jer. So.

Soon our Prep is set I even have *bathrobe*.

The door knocks.

He's so tired, Meg says to a lady coming in with second lady with *camera*.

We may need to keep this brief, says Jer.

He took a crazy bad beating, Meg says.

As you saw, says Kennedy B.

As all of us saw, Jer says.

As the whole world saw, Meg says. Nice old guy, just trying to voice his views, gets his free speech denied?

What have we come to? says Kennedy B.

Just wrong, says Meg.

Lady: And you folks are?

Niece, says Meg.

Niece also, says Kennedy B.

Nephew, says Jer.

Lights in my face.

Blink, blink.

Lady gives me look of love And her voice changes to smooth and sympathy.

Tell me, Greg, she says. Why, at your age, would you feel compelled to join the protests? When you could be sitting comfortably here in this lovely home, enjoying your retirement or gardening, if you enjoy gardening, as so many old folks seem to? Not to appear ageist? Or playing cards or watching old movies on TV?

I care about this country, I say.

(As Prepped.)

Jer and Meg and Kennedy B. look at me like: Yes, yes, how well said, by our uncle.

I believe I should be able to state my views, though old, I say.

So true, says Kennedy B.

So modestly put, says Meg.

Remember that time he anonymously paid my college tuition? says Kennedy B.

That time he donated his Buick to the Park District? says Meg. Anonymously?

On a more serious note, to somewhat shift gears, the lady says. There are rumors afloat of a secret cadre of folks who are, one might say, mind-washed, or sort of like zombies who just show up? Individuals blanked out mentally, then reprogrammed — human robots, so to speak — who arrive en masse, even in buses, for propaganda purposes?

Silence.

I did not understand what you just said, please explain, I say.

He gets confused so easily, Meg says. These days. At his age.

When he was younger? Jer says. Never confused. Sharp as a tack.

Just one sharp uncle, says Kennedy B.

Of ours, says Meg.

And that darn beating probably didn't help much, says Kennedy B.

Have you, Greg, to the best of your recollection, received any training or programming of this kind? the lady says. Can you name, for example, the place of your birth?

Meg touches her hat.

Special high school memories? the lady says. A show you enjoyed as a child? Who are you, Greg? In what do you, yourself, believe?

Freedom, I say. For *poor* and *sick.* And defend *weak* from *oppressors.*

Ha, oh boy, the lady says. That is rich. Defend the weak? Allentown, Pennsylvania, Greg: ring a bell? Certain brutal events that occurred there to some union-organizer folks in a mini-mall? Galena, Illinois, what transpired there, tragically, last July, to a group of unarmed middle school teachers?

Meg touches her hat, clears throat.

What is your last name, Greg? the lady says. Do you even know it? The approximate year of the moon landing? The name of the football team from Cleveland? How is it that this house was rented only three days ago? Why, when you fellows chant, do you always chant the same four words?

Meg clears throat, widens eyes, touches hat.

Bastard, turd, creep, idiot, the lady says.

I hop up, excuse self, go to bathroom.

You call yourself a journalist? Kennedy B. says.

You call yourself a person? the lady says.

I wait in bathroom until ladies, *camera,* leave.

Cat in *tub* Curled up happy Why O why cannot I be more like it? Not confused Just curled up My tub making my purr be louder.

Jer comes in closes door leans against.

Okay, that was unfortunate, Jer says. That lady? Janet Ardmore, KTODNews-TeamTwo? Stinker. Real crankypants. Kind of biased. Strange view of the world. Bit of a liar. Funny how badness will just say whatever, you know? But, I admit, we're in a bind. And, no offense: you are one shit interview, pal.

I do not understand what you just said, please explain, I say.

Door flies open Meg and Kennedy B. squeeze in Jer steps into tub with slight look of *yikes.*

Cat races out.

Jer, KZIP's calling and calling, says Meg. KDUC's parked right up the frigging street. In that yellow van. With the beak on it.

I do not understand what you just said, please explain, I say.

You know what, 89? says Meg. You're going to stop saying that. You're driving me freaking nuts with that.

Meg's stressed, says Jer.

We're all stressed, says Kennedy B.

Contrary to popular belief, I am not some bitch made of stone, says Meg.

I never said you were a bitch made of

stone, says Kennedy B. I said you could sometimes be a very company lady.

Glimm's on his way over, says Meg. With the portable. Right? Totally works: we Re-scrape. Per the QAPP. Which we should've done long ago. It's brain damage. We say. To whoever. From the beating. See? Win-win. Afterward, 89's subdued and blank. Can't speak. At all. Who did it? Them. They did. Beat a nice old guy so bad they blanked him right out. And they call themselves moral? Like that.

What a shame, says Jer. Total waste of a year.

He has to consent, Kennedy B. says soft ly handing Meg a *page* by hand.

Are you sad, pal, are you scared, do you know what's about to happen? says Jer.

The time for delicate feelings is I don't know when, says Meg. But not now.

Miles and miles up shit creek here, says Kennedy B.

And just like snap at her word of *creek* I know *creek*: is that is that which at edge of which we would build *ramp* of *snow snow-ramp* If jump no good? Boy and *sled* fell in *creek* Boy must run home, pants of *ice,* dragging *sled* Pants getting more *ice* with each cold step through quiet blue winter town toward home sweet

Ma, I think.

Then see her so clear: *Flour* in hair Mouth going O at sight of *icepants* Which I am to leave by door on *Hefty bag,* spread out Here is *Vixen* Our *dog!* Sniffing my *icepants* which I am no longer which lie now on *Hefty bag* In shape of boy doing dance one leg bent.

Jer leans against sink Makes desk of own back Meg puts page on Jer's backdesk hands me pen.

So 89, this is just going to be your CF-201B, Meg says. Addendum to your CF-201A. Which you already signed. Happily. Gladly. Earlier.

When you first joined us, says Kennedy B.

Joined our team, says Meg.

It doesn't hurt, 89, says Kennedy B. Remember? It's just with magnets and whatnot?

How would he remember that, doofus? says Meg.

He seems to actually remember kind of a lot, says Kennedy B.

If I ever lied to you, 89, which I didn't? Jer says. Or deceived you? Or withheld or misrepresented certain information? It was for your own good. To make your life better.

Jer, why are you even going there right

304

now? says Meg.

Sometimes, to do good, there are steps along the way at which goodness must be temporarily set aside or lost sight of, says Jer.

Hooray, says Meg. Good meeting.

Make your X, 89, says Jer.

Maybe now we can get out of this stupid tiny bathroom at least, says Kennedy B.

I love that idea so much, says Meg.

Carol, I say.

What's that, 89? says Jer.

Carol Spencer, I say. Carol K. Spencer.

Ah, shit, says Meg. Perfect.

Carol K. Spencer, 1539 Becker Street, Schenectady, New York, I say. 12304.

Then place pen in sink Polite ly.

Per Meg Jer takes me into *yard* For *frank urgent pep talk pronto.*

This, right now, 89? says Jer. *Dusk.* That there? *Aspen.* Over there? *Storage shed. Gate. Sunflowers.* This thing blowing? *Breeze.* Check that out. Up there. Did you even know that was a thing?

Sun and *moon* in sky at once.

You seem agitated, pal, says Jer. Standoffish. Not your usual peppy self.

I blink.

Would like to visit, I say.

305

Visit what? Jer says.

Ma, I say.

Ha, wow, interesting, Jer says. Bargaining. Pretty advanced. Is that your, uh, demand, 89? Like, pre-signing demand? We take you to see your mother, you sign?

Yes? I say.

I'm going to level with you, 89, Jer says. Have we done *level with you*? Figure of speech?

Tell the truth, I say.

Remember when we had all those moths back at Room Valiant? Jer says. And sprayed? And they were, like, lying all over everything? Not moving? And we swept them up and bagged them up and all of that? Those moths? Were *dead.* Had *died.* Perfectly normal. Remember Gladys? Who used to clean Room Valiant? Remember when Gladys started no longer coming in? A person reaches a certain age.

No spring chicken, I say.

Exactly, Jer says. Happens to everybody. Even you. Even me. Our mothers, even. I mean, think about it, 89, how old are you? Seventy-five, eighty? Your mother would, of course, be older.

Low over yard comes V of birds.

Geese, says Jer. That sound? *Honk.*

The *honks* go deeper, lower as *geese* fly

farther further One *geese* falls behind Flies funnily faster until back home again in his or her V.

My mother is *death*? I say.

Ha, no, your mother is not *death,* 89, Jer says. She is *dead.* Has *died.* Is how we might say that one. Sorry. Sorry for your loss. Must be painful. To forget your mother existed, then remember she existed, then right away find out she's all of a sudden dead? Ouch. I thought I had it bad, when I knew all along my mom existed and then she died. But, sadly, this is the type of painful thing that occurs when a person gets a subpar Scrape.

Level with me, I say.

Just did, says Jer.

Again, I say.

We're crazy tight on time, 89, Jer says.

How did I get here? I say.

Back door swings open Shape of light runs out *Lightshape* To Jer Jer's shoes Which light up With light.

Glimm's here, says Kennedy B., leaning out of door. He needs help. With the portable. My back is shit and Meg's back is shit. So.

Kennedy B. goes back in, door swings shut.

Lightshape follows.

Yard dark.

Speaking again, or still, of *death,* 89? Jer says. Look how weird and slow you walk. How short of breath. Are you entirely well, totally young? We, as a company, paid for a routine physical. Charitably. For all you folks living under that bridge. For lots of folks, living under a number of bridges, across a number of states. Results, for you? Not great. So you said, intelligently, to yourself, Hey, do I want to sicken and die under this bridge over the next ten to eighteen months, in the company of those same creeps who have bullied me and treated me like shit most of my adult life, or go live somewhere safe out west, with killer meals and free meds and a team of young colleagues who'll watch over me and maybe even put some purpose back into my life?

Blink.

Here's what the QAPP says, Jer says. *In the event of a subpar Scrape, should Associate refuse recommended Rescrape, Associate is to be removed from Program immediately and restored to his or her Locale of Origin,* which, for you, brother, means: we ship you back east and plop you under that same old bridge, among the fighting and the smoke and the filth and your same old nasty pals. Which is something I don't cherish doing to someone I've come to respect and, to be frank, even love.

Blink.

Sorry to be so blunt, 89, says Jer. But that's what friends are for.

The night is now a big night in its sky: low, blue, black stars all in a smear.

Sun gone moon winning.

Moon has won.

From inside house, someone Glimm maybe *coughs.*

Cat in window looks out tail swishing head tilted as if to say: *Why not have me for your cat, 89?*

Sad sad though:

If *blankslate* that sledding boy those blue-white days that flour-haired *Ma?*

Gone.

And no one left to remember them ever again.

No one left to remember *Ma* bringing my *blue robe* wrapping me up.

My sweet little man she says Imagine the lovely things you will someday achieve in this magnificent world How proud you will make me, your mother.

O *Ma* O sorry *Ma* did not achieve any lovely in this magnificent

Back door swings open.

Lightshape runs out.

Meg steps around Kennedy B. comes off *porch* crosses *yard* walking odd ly high *heels* on wet *grass* kisses me on *cheek* puts flower in my pocket.

Rose, Kennedy B. says from *porch.* Means she loves you.

Well, I actually sort of do, says Meg.

Come on, 89, sweetie, let's go inside, says Kennedy B. Next thing you know, you wake up fresh, whole new start.

No more looking backward, 89, says Jer. Only forward. From now on.

With us, says Kennedy B. Your friends.

Until the end, says Jer.

Doesn't that sound nice, 89? says Meg.

Yes, I say.

But can we give a few secs? I say.

Can *we* give *you* a few secs, says Jer.

Can you give me a few secs? I say.

Not sure why we're getting super wonky over syntax this late in the game, says Meg.

It's sweet, he wants some me time, says Kennedy B.

They cross yard open door *lightshape* runs out.

Lightshape runs back in.

Am alone in yard.

Smear of stars widest, lowest yet *Aspens*

sway *Storage shed* makes *frog* noise with each *breeze.*

Must think take my few secs to

I am not am not now am no longer Elliott Spencer exactly.

The me I am now has never been *wino* has never had *wine* does not want since never has had.

The me I am now has words memories new and old I like him who I am like him fine do not wish to lose him or his memories of Ma or memories of *Vixen* of my old school *St. Damian's clang* in *breeze* goes *flagpole rope* against *flagpole Vincent* brings *sugarstraw* for me in his *mitten* and *sugarstraw* for him in his other green *mitten* Because we are: *blood brothers.*

Far from home Ma *dead.*

Have no *friend* or *pal* in all of world.

Breeze now more *Aspens* shake crazy in their *leaves Gate* clicks its *latch* with each new push of *breeze.*

And just like snap I know: Ma's *gate* was missing one *hinge* must be careful when the way to be careful when opening Ma's gate is use both hands Much fun in Ma's yard So many wild

Ma holding *picnic basket* rushes over

whacks me with *basket* I laugh and laugh and

Ruth is there Ha, *Ruth*! I recall you! O pretty *Ruth* lies at base of tree I just have am *blotto* have just knocked *Ruth* right *Ruth,* on ground, holding *stuffed bear* I gave her: You break my heart, Elliott, I wouldn't marry you if you were the last

Ma: El, sweet Jesus. You drink and drink and do such crazy

Grab *bear* from *Ruth* throw *bear* on *grill.*

Bear burning *ring* I bought Ruth still taped to *paw.*

Look at you, idiot! *Ma* says. Is that who you are? Give me those goddamn keys.

Go out gate to my *Electra brand-new Electra.*

Ma drops gray head so sad Helps *Ruth* up. Blink.

Little sick, recalling that.

Is that man me, now? Would I, man I am now, knock down *Ruth,* throw *bear* on *grill,* get in *Electra,* drive to *Tom's Dizzy Oasis,* get further *blotto*?

No.

If I could go back in yard? Would take bear from fire Pull ring off bear Give ring to Ruth, saying: Ruth, sorry, let us love each other forever.

But Ruth married *Philip,* moved far away

312

I recall I now recall.

If Ruth not gone Ma not *death* I would say: Ruth, Ma, the me I was then is not the only me I may ever There is a me under that me who yet wishes to do lovely in this magnificent

Watch, Ruth: Watch, Ma: This new me in what time he has left?

Will try.

I go through *gate* using both hands Am out of *yard* into (ha ha, I now recall it): *lot vacant lot* Never have I been so alone with myself while outside! knees hurt no spring chicken.

When will I *death*? Might I *death* alone? Probably yes Little scared about that. I must say

But am not *death* yet

Not *dead* yet.

Not yet.

And not yet.

World lays out before me new with each click of step and swish of aspen leaves above for that I say thanks For as long as world is shiny new there is no *death* and what lovely may I not yet do?

Here is *cactus* Word I know from long-ago *cartoons* watched with *Ma* These *west* trees (I know like snap) are not my old *east* trees that I knew by heart: *sycamore, dog-*

wood, beech I do not, as yet, know *west's*
trees' names *western* trees' names But will
will soon can learn am learning all the time.
Know: *night, star, moon*
Know: *walk,* know *hide*
Know: *path* and little bit smiling take it.

MY HOUSE

Who would sell a gem like that? Well, Mel Hays. That was his name. Per Jordan at Hillside Realty. He was mad to sell. Sick wife, had just retired, couldn't keep the place up. Odd duck, Jordan said, required a personal meeting with anyone thinking of offering.

My God, we hit it off. Hays was big, shaggy, friendly, funny: the brother I'd never had. He'd worked for the village, had a thing for history. Me too, I said, and we shared a mutual history-nerd blush. What I loved about the place were exactly the things he loved about it: the barn (built in 1789); the six leaning hitching posts, each capped with a different serpent face; the oak from which the wrong man had been hung for treason; the smaller oak planted over the spot where the man's body lay buried for fifteen years before his family came to dig him up.

Ghosts? I asked.

Ho ho, he said, touching my arm, meaning: There's more to say on that matter, friend.

The door to the room where the wife was sick stayed closed. But the rest of the house, Good Lord. Bookshelves everywhere, of mahogany and maple, strange half-rooms stuffed with cased artifacts: a Tahitian oar, the neck of a fiddle played at Antietam, a child's jacket from the time of Washington, smudged, just there, with mud from the period.

Amazing, I said.

We've been lucky, he said.

The interior showed signs of the neglect associated with the wife's illness and their shortage of funds and I resolved, in the name of this surprising warmth between us, to meet his asking price.

Just because.

Because I had it.

By the time we came back out onto the wide porch I had so admired from the road we were friends and the house, it seemed, was mine. There's a family of foxes who come to sit over there in the arbor, he said. And: Those dogwoods flower white like crazy in early April. And: You'll want to watch the basement walls for cracks in the winter.

It had a manor-house feeling and sat high on a hill overlooking the quaint little village.

I thought of my friends moving awed through the wide front hall, craning their necks up that mysterious winding stairwell, and then I'd guide them upstairs to the room where, in such-and-such a year, So-and-so had endured a difficult childbirth. I'd do research on the house and compile my findings in a leather-bound book, to be placed in the pentagonal recess in the narrow hall that led to the former servants' quarters. All my life I'd believed I'd some-day live in a place like this, had suffered the distance between such places as they existed in my imagination and the places in which I'd actually lived (before Kay, with Kay, after Kay left): their low ceilings, ugly heat vents, hollow pine doors. To live here would be, I imagined, a sort of exorcism of all the limitations I'd ever felt. Here one sensed — craftsmanship, yes, but also, my God — the past, the living past: the parties held, the food served, the dust motes of 1862, the war goodbyes of 1917, the whispered late-night dramas that had forever altered the lives of the people who'd once moved down these very hallways and now lay buried in the village graveyard I'd visited on the way over, trailing my hands over the mossy stones, reading names aloud, thinking, Poor bastards, you no longer walk in the sun.

Hays paused us at an orchard. Apples and pears had once hung thick on the trees and carpeted the ground, he said. Now, well, no. There was some sort of disease. He'd been preoccupied.

And he gestured up at the window of the sickroom of the wife.

I'll hire a gardener, I thought, get it back to health. He seemed to read my mind and the look on his face said: You showing up here, now, to steward this beloved place, and with the means to do so, proves that such a thing as good fortune truly exists.

Our handshake seemed to mean: Let's burn through the technicalities, get the thing done.

It kills me, he said. To think of losing this place forever.

I get that, I said.

And I did. My mind leapt ahead, to that sad future someday when I, too, would lose it forever.

It's heaven, he said. It's been a heaven for the two of us.

I believe it, I said.

Maybe, he said, and a look came over his

face, a self-doubting look, and I found myself wanting to offer whatever he needed.

It was strange, very strange, to like someone so much on a first meeting.

Go on, I said.

Maybe I could drop by now and then, he said.

And I thought: Well, yes, sure, it would be good to see him once in a while.

But then he went on.

Spend a day or two, he said. Stay in the guest room, maybe.

I didn't say no. I didn't. But a look must have passed over my face. Wouldn't a look have passed over yours? Dropping by . . . well, maybe. But spending "a day or two"? "In the guest room"? Did he mean my guest room or theirs? The room they had designated or the one I soon would —

It was one too many, somehow.

Then I thought: He won't take me up on it once he's out; he's just talking, to be comforted.

Recovering my manners, I said yes, of course he would be welcome, they would, always welcome, anytime at all.

But now there was a look on his face.

Anytime at all, I said. Truly.

He gave me a pat on the back, said we'd see how things went, made a vague, despair-

319

ing gesture at my car, as in: There it is, you know where it is, off you go.

I thought: Too bad. But, then again, where is it written we have to be friends?

I sat in the car awhile, looking up at the house, already loving it more than I'd ever loved any place in my life.

I called Jordan, had her make the full-price offer, plus ten percent. Next morning, she called back, mystified. It seemed he'd changed his mind. About selling. It was the oddest thing, she said. No way he could afford to keep the place. His agent said the same. Together, they were trying to figure out what the hell had gone wrong. Hays was on a tiny pension, his wife was dying, there were medical bills, the house had been on the market for two years, mine was the first offer.

Did you say something? she asked. Do something?

He said he sometimes might want to come and stay over, I said. Like, overnight. And I just, you know, hesitated.

That's weird, she said. I mean, sounds like you were well within your rights.

I think so, I said. I didn't say no. I just . . .

And that did it? she said. Wow.

We went back, offered more, then more, until, finally, we were offering more than a third again above his original asking price.

But it was still a no.

In January the wife died. I sent a condolence card, with an offer to meet for coffee, got no response. I started driving by now and then just to torture myself. That spring, the roof of the side library collapsed after a tree fell on it. Soon the tree had become part of the house. After a heavy summer rain, the front porch I'd loved so much sank into the earth a foot or so on the south end; three of its columns bowed and cracked. Then one gave way and the two halves of it lay in the yard and the lip of the roof there drooped and you could see into the rusty, filth-packed gutter. By October the grand front lawn was overgrown and wild turkeys were foraging there. You'd see them, big and ugly, strutting around like dinosaurs.

Some nights a single light showed from an upstairs window.

Finally I wrote him a letter. Was there not some way to fix this? Wasn't it in our mutual interest to talk the thing through, come to some agreement? I got no answer, wrote another. We're both good people, I wrote, this is a win-win, can't we let bygones be bygones? I am deeply sorry, I said, that I did not respond more generously in the moment. I was just taken aback. Briefly. I didn't say no, after all; I only hesitated. Was that an unforgivable sin? Surely a person could forgive the mistake of an instant?

Nothing.

A third letter: Wasn't he ashamed of himself, for being so obstinate? Was this not, what we two old men were enacting, exactly what has ailed the world since time immemorial? Did he really think it was appropriate to make the sale of a property contingent on installing himself as a sort of permanent possible houseguest? What sort of dream world was he living in?

No answer.

A fourth: You'll die, I'll get the house, trust me. Why not sell now? Use the money to live a better life than the tormented one it would appear you are living, sitting up there lonely and bitter, letting that beautiful place, a place you loved, a place the two of you loved, go to seed. Shame on you, I hope you're enjoying the fruits of your arrogance, you stubborn, mean-spirited old bastard.

That one, to my credit, I never sent. I wadded it up, burned it over the stove.

I had fallen ill. I am ill now. My time is short. I burned that letter to prepare myself to face what is coming with as pure a heart as I can manage.

I need to write another. Of course. I know

that. If only for my own benefit.

I am truly sorry, it will begin. Sorry for my part in this. What did you deny me, really, after all? A beautiful year or so, in a lovely place. It would have made me happy. But what is it, a year, in the grand scheme? Nothing. What are ten years, a hundred, a thousand? I am going, friend, I am all but gone, I believe you prideful and wrong but I have no desire, now, to cure you. Your wrongness was an idea I had. I am all but gone. My idea of your wrongness will go with me. Your rightness is an idea you are having. It will go with you. For all of that, I hope you live forever, and if the place falls down around you, as it seems to be doing, I hope even that brings you joy. It was always falling down around you, everything has always been falling down around us. Only we were too alive to notice. I feel the truth of this in my body now. I am trying not to be terrified. But I am sometimes, in the night. If you are a praying man, pray for me, friend. Friend who might have been. Friend who should have been.

That letter exists in my mind. But I am too tired to write it. Well, that is not true. I am not too tired.

I'm just not ready.

The surge of pride and life and self is still

too strong in me.

But I will get there. I will. I will write it yet.

Only I must not wait too long.

ABOUT THE AUTHOR

George Saunders is the author of twelve books, including *Lincoln in the Bardo,* which debuted at #1 on the *New York Times* bestseller list, won the 2017 Man Booker Prize for best work of fiction in English, and was a finalist for the Golden Man Booker, in which one Booker winner was selected to represent each decade, from the fifty years since the prize's inception. The audiobook for *Lincoln in the Bardo,* which features a cast of 166 actors, won the 2018 Audie Award for best audiobook. The story collection *Tenth of December* was a finalist for the National Book Award; it won the inaugural Folio Prize in 2013 (for the best work of fiction in English) and the Story Prize. Saunders has received MacArthur and Guggenheim fellowships and the PEN/Malamud Prize for Excellence in the Short Story. In 2013, he was named one of the world's one hundred most influential people by *Time* magazine. He has taught in the creative writing program at Syracuse University since 1997.

The employees of Thorndike Press hope you have enjoyed this Large Print book. All our Thorndike, Wheeler, and Kennebec Large Print titles are designed for easy reading, and all our books are made to last. Other Thorndike Press Large Print books are available at your library, through selected bookstores, or directly from us.

For information about titles, please call:
(800) 223-1244

or visit our website at:
gale.com/thorndike

To share your comments, please write:
Publisher
Thorndike Press
10 Water St., Suite 310
Waterville, ME 04901